Unlocking Life's Secrets: A Journey to True Meaning

BY

KANIKA GUPTA

ISBN (Paperback): 978-93-343-0549-4
ISBN (Ebook): 978-93-343-2863-9

First Edition: June 2025

Disclaimer:
This is a work of creative fictitious. Some names, characters, places, and incidents may be drawn from real experiences or imagination. Any resemblance to actual persons, living or deceased, is coincidental.
Author asserts moral right to be identified as the author of this work.

Cover design by Vinay Gupta
Interior design by Self

Publisher: Self

Contents

Preface

In a world that often feels fragmented, chaotic, and overwhelming, the quest for stability is more profound than ever. We are constantly searching—sometimes consciously, sometimes unconsciously—for meaning, peace, and connection in our lives. It was this universal yearning that inspired me to write this book, a story about three extraordinary yet relatable individuals who embark on transformative journeys toward inner harmony.

Vivaan Gupta, a hardworking corporate professional caught in the relentless grind of deadlines and expectations; Bharat Mathur, a retired professor grappling with the quiet void left by years of structured academia; and Saachi, a resilient single mother navigating life's challenges while striving to create a better future for her child—all find themselves at crossroads. Each carries their own burdens, fears, and unanswered questions. Yet, through serendipity or perhaps destiny, they discover meditation as a pathway to something far greater: becoming one with Universal Consciousness.

This book is not just a narrative—it's an invitation. An invitation to pause, reflect, and explore what it means to be truly connected—not only to ourselves but also to the universe around us. Through the stories of Vivaan, Bharat, and Saachi, we witness how mindfulness and meditation can transcend barriers of age, profession, and circumstance. Their experiences remind us that no matter where we come from or what challenges we face, the essence of who we are remains unchanged, infinite, and eternal.

As you turn these pages, I hope you'll see reflections of your own journey in theirs. Perhaps you'll recognize moments when you've felt lost, uncertain, or burdened by life's weight. And perhaps, like them, you'll begin to uncover the tools within yourself to rise above those struggles and embrace a deeper sense of purpose and belonging.

Writing this book has been my way of exploring humanity's shared longing for unity and understanding. It is my belief that each of us possesses a unique spark—a light that connects us to something vast and infinite. My wish is that "Unlocking Life's Secrets" serves as a guiding light for anyone seeking solace, inspiration, or simply a reminder that they are never alone.

With gratitude and love,

Kanika Gupta

Chapter 1: The Whisper of Curiosity

The late afternoon sun filtered through the dusty windowpanes of Vivaan Gupta's modest flat in Pitampura, North Delhi. The neighborhood buzzed with life—children playing cricket on the narrow streets, vendors calling out their wares, and the occasional honk of an auto-rickshaw weaving its way through the chaos. Yet inside Vivaan's home, there was a quiet stillness that contrasted sharply with the world outside.

Vivaan sat at the dining table, savoring the last bites of a freshly prepared meal. Unnati, his wife, had made one of his favorites—dal makhani with jeera rice and a side of crispy papad. As always, she insisted on serving him first, ensuring he ate hot, fresh food before it cooled. Leftovers were never an option in their household; Unnati took pride in feeding her family wholesome meals every day, no matter how busy life got.

Across the room, their nine-year-old daughter, Shanaya, sprawled on the carpet, engrossed in her sketchbook, humming softly to herself. She occasionally glanced up to steal a piece of papad from Vivaan's plate, giggling when he playfully scolded her. "Daddy's dear daughter needs energy too!" she declared, popping the crispy bite into her mouth.

For years, Vivaan had prided himself on being the backbone of his family—the dependable CPA who worked tirelessly for a foreign multinational corporation to provide for everyone he loved. He believed in simple living and high thinking, finding joy in small moments: Unnati's lovingly cooked meals, Shanaya's infectious laughter, or quiet evenings spent together as a family. But despite his efforts to live authentically, he often felt like an outsider in the high-class society of Pitampura.

At social gatherings hosted by colleagues or neighbors, Vivaan was constantly reminded of what he lacked—a luxury car, a sprawling apartment, designer clothes. Neighbors whispered behind his back, questioning why someone working for a foreign MNC lived so modestly. Even Unnati sometimes urged him to be more assertive, though she admired his gentle nature.

The only person who truly saw him for who he was—and adored him unconditionally—was Shanaya. To her, he wasn't just a provider; he was her hero. She called him "Daddy" with such reverence that it melted away all his frustrations. When she ran up to him after school, clutching a drawing she'd made of them together, or when she tucked herself under his arm during movie nights, Vivaan felt like the richest man alive.

Yet, lately, even these moments couldn't dispel the growing emptiness inside him. Despite his best efforts to stay grounded,

Vivaan couldn't shake the feeling that something was missing. Perhaps it was the constant tug-of-war between his values and the world's expectations. Or maybe it was the gnawing sense that he was meant for something more than balancing ledgers and attending endless meetings.

His phone buzzed on the table, snapping him out of his reverie. It was a message from work—a reminder about an upcoming deadline. Vivaan sighed and set the phone aside, glancing at the pile of mail Unnati had placed on the table earlier. Amidst utility bills and bank statements, one envelope stood out. It was plain white, with no return address, just his name written in bold black ink: Vivaan Gupta. Something about it caught his eye, perhaps the faint scent of sandalwood wafting from the paper when he picked it up.

Curiosity tugged at him, and after a moment's hesitation, he tore open the seal. Inside was a single sheet of parchment, its edges slightly frayed, as if it had traveled through time itself. The handwriting was elegant yet cryptic:

"To find what you seek, look where shadows dance and truths lie buried. Begin with the name 'Radha.' Time is fleeting; do not wait."

Vivaan froze, his breath catching in his throat. Who could have sent this? And what did it mean? Radha? The name stirred something deep within him, though he couldn't place why. Shadows danced... truths buried... It sounded like the beginning of a riddle, one that promised answers to questions Vivaan hadn't even dared to ask."Papa, what's that?" Shanaya asked, looking up from her sketchbook. Her wide brown eyes sparkled with curiosity.

"It's nothing, beta," Vivaan said quickly, folding the letter and slipping it into his pocket. But the words lingered in his mind, gnawing at him.

Later that evening, as Unnati busied herself in the kitchen preparing masala chai, and Shanaya practiced her multiplication tables aloud, Vivaan found himself staring out the window at the fading light. The city stretched endlessly before him, alive with color and noise. For the first time in months—or maybe years—he allowed himself to imagine a life beyond spreadsheets and boardroom meetings. This simple act of curiosity might lead him somewhere unexpected, somewhere meaningful.

But how could he pursue this mystery without upsetting the delicate balance of his responsibilities? Between work, family, and societal expectations, Vivaan had spent decades putting others' needs ahead of his own desires. Yet the letter seemed to whisper that it wasn't too late to change—to uncover hidden truths not just about himself, but about the legacy of his family.

Little did he know, this decision would set off a chain reaction that would alter not only his life but the lives of those around him.

Chapter 2: The Threads of Connection

The morning sun filtered through the cracked blinds of a small, one-bedroom flat in West Delhi, casting long streaks of light across the cluttered living room. Saachi Sharma sat cross-legged on the floor, her laptop balanced precariously on her knees as she scrolled through job listings. Her dark hair was tied back in a loose bun, strands escaping to frame her tired face. She sighed, closing the lid of the laptop with a sense of defeat.

At thirty-two, Saachi had spent the last decade juggling the roles of mother, caregiver, and breadwinner. Her son, Atharv, now eight years old, was the center of her world. But raising him alone after her husband walked out five years ago had left her stretched thin—emotionally, financially, and physically. Every day felt like a battle: waking up before dawn to prepare breakfast for Atharv, dropping him off at school, then rushing to whatever part-time gig she could find to make ends meet.

Yet, despite the exhaustion, Saachi couldn't help but feel a deep longing for something more. It wasn't just financial stability she craved—it was connection. A sense of belonging. Someone who truly understood the weight she carried and could share the burden, if only for a moment.

Her phone buzzed on the table beside her, pulling her from her thoughts. It was a message from her best friend, Priya: "You need to take care of yourself too, yaar. When was the last time you did something just for YOU?"

Saachi stared at the screen, her throat tightening. She wanted to respond, to say that she deserved happiness, that she would find time for herself someday. But the words wouldn't come. Instead, she tucked the phone back into her bag and turned her attention to the pile of laundry waiting to be folded. Life didn't stop for self-reflection—not when there were bills to pay and a child to raise.

Meanwhile, across town in East Delhi, Bharat Mathur sat on the balcony of his modest apartment, sipping a cup of steaming chai as he watched the city wake up below. At sixty-four, retirement should have been a time of relaxation and reflection. But for Bharat, it felt more like a void—a gaping hole where purpose used to reside.

For over three decades, Bharat had been a beloved teacher at a local government school, shaping young minds and instilling in them a love for learning. He'd poured his heart into his work, often staying late to tutor struggling students or counsel those dealing with personal challenges. Now, without the structure of teaching, he found himself adrift. His wife had passed away two years ago, leaving behind an emptiness that no amount of solitude could fill.

Bharat missed the connections he once had—the laughter of children filling the classroom, the gratitude in a parent's eyes when their child succeeded. He missed feeling needed. These days, his interactions were limited to brief exchanges with neighbors or the occasional phone call from his daughter, who lived abroad. Though she tried to stay in touch, the distance between them felt insurmountable.

As he finished his tea, Bharat noticed a flyer taped to the building's notice board. It advertised a community storytelling event at a nearby library—a chance for people to share stories about their lives and experiences. Something about it caught his interest. Maybe it was the promise of human connection, however fleeting. Or maybe it was the idea that his own story might still matter to someone.

He tore off one of the flyers and slipped it into his pocket, resolving to attend. For the first time in months, he felt a flicker of hope—a possibility that life wasn't entirely behind him yet.

Unbeknownst to both Saachi and Bharat, their paths were destined to cross with Vivaan's in ways none of them could foresee. Each of them carried their own burdens, their own yearnings for meaning and connection. And though they moved through different corners of the bustling city, their lives were threads in the same intricate tapestry—a reminder that no one is truly alone, even in moments of profound isolation.

For now, however, they remained unaware of each other. Saachi continued her search for stability, clinging to the hope that things would get better for Atharv. Bharat prepared to step out of his comfort zone, seeking solace in shared stories. And Vivaan, tucked away in Pitampura, clutched the mysterious letter in his pocket, wondering what secrets it held—and whether following its clues might lead him closer to understanding not just himself, but the invisible bonds that connected all of humanity.

Little did any of them know, the journey ahead would challenge everything they thought they knew about themselves and each other.

Chapter 3: The Puzzle of the Past

The next morning, Vivaan woke earlier than usual, the mysterious letter still tucked safely in his pocket. He had spent most of the night tossing and turning, the cryptic message replaying in his mind like a broken record: "To find what you seek, look where shadows dance and truths lie buried. Begin with the name 'Radha.' Time is fleeting; do not wait."

As he sipped his morning tea on the balcony, the city below slowly came to life. Rickshaws rattled down the streets, vendors set up their carts, and children hurried to school in neatly pressed uniforms. Vivaan watched it all with a sense of detachment, his thoughts consumed by the riddle. What did it mean? And why did the name Radha feel so familiar, yet elusive?

Unnati joined him a few minutes later, carrying a tray with fresh parathas and curd. "You seem distracted," she said softly, placing the tray on the small table between them. "Is everything okay?"

Vivaan hesitated, debating whether to share the letter with her. But something held him back—a gut feeling that this was his journey to embark on alone, at least for now. "It's nothing," he replied with a faint smile. "Just work stress."

Unnati studied him for a moment, then nodded, accepting his answer without pressing further. She knew better than to push when Vivaan retreated into himself. Instead, she changed the subject, asking about Shanaya's upcoming school project. Vivaan listened half-heartedly, his mind still circling back to the letter.

After breakfast, Unnati left to run errands, and Shanaya went to her room to practice piano. Vivaan seized the opportunity to examine the letter more closely. He spread it out on the dining table, tracing the elegant handwriting with his fingers. Shadows dance... truths buried... Begin with the name Radha.

A memory stirred deep within him, vague but persistent. He remembered sitting on his grandmother's lap as a child, listening to her stories about their ancestors. One name stood out— Radha. His grandmother had mentioned her only once, describing her as a distant relative who had disappeared under mysterious circumstances decades ago. At the time, Vivaan had been too young to understand the significance, but now the pieces began falling into place.

Determined to learn more, Vivaan rummaged through the old wooden trunk in the storeroom where his parents kept family heirlooms and documents. Dust clung to his hands as he sifted through faded photographs, brittle letters, and yellowed certificates. Finally, he found what he was looking for—a leather-bound journal belonging to his great-grandfather.

The journal's pages were filled with handwritten entries detailing the family's history. Flipping through them, Vivaan discovered references to Radha—a woman described as intelligent, spirited, and fiercely independent. According to the journal, she had left home during the Partition of India in 1947, seeking refuge in another country. Her decision had caused a rift in the family, and over time, her name became taboo, rarely spoken aloud.

Vivaan felt a pang of sadness as he read about Radha's struggles and ultimate disappearance. It was as if a part of their family's story had been erased, leaving behind unanswered questions and unresolved pain. He realized that understanding Radha's fate might hold the key to unraveling the mystery of the letter—and perhaps his own sense of purpose.

Meanwhile, miles away in West Delhi, Saachi sat on the edge of her bed, staring at an old photograph of her late father. It was his birthday, a day she always marked privately, even years after his passing. In the photo, he stood beside her mother, both smiling brightly despite the hardships they faced raising a family in a cramped chawl.

Memories flooded back—her father teaching her how to ride a bicycle, his laughter echoing through the narrow alleys as she wobbled unsteadily. Later, when her parents' marriage fell apart, her father became her anchor, offering quiet support while shielding her from the chaos. After his sudden death from a heart attack, Saachi vowed to carry forward the values he instilled in her: resilience, kindness, and an unwavering belief in the goodness of people.

But life hadn't turned out the way she imagined. The weight of single parenthood often left her questioning whether she was living up to her father's legacy. As she tucked the photograph back into its frame, Saachi whispered a silent prayer, asking for strength to keep going—for Atharv's sake, if nothing else.

In East Delhi, Bharat sat in his favorite armchair, flipping through a photo album he hadn't opened in years. The images transported him back to his days as a teacher—the classroom decorated with colorful charts, the eager faces of students listening intently as he explained complex concepts. Among the photos was one of a young girl named Meera, one of his brightest pupils who had overcome immense personal challenges to excel academically.

Meera's story had stayed with him long after she graduated. Abandoned by her parents, she had grown up in a shelter, relying on scholarships and sheer determination to build a better future. Bharat had mentored her tirelessly, watching with pride as she secured admission to a prestigious university. Yet, somewhere along the way, they lost touch. He wondered what had become of her—whether she had achieved her dreams or succumbed to the harsh realities of life.

Closing the album, Bharat felt a renewed determination to reconnect with the world outside his solitude. Perhaps attending the storytelling event wasn't just about finding connection—it was about honoring the impact he'd had on others and rediscovering his own worth.

Unbeknownst to Vivaan, Saachi, and Bharat, their individual quests for truth and meaning were threads in a larger tapestry. Each of them carried fragments of the past—family legacies, personal losses, and unspoken hopes—that would eventually intertwine, revealing hidden connections none of them could have anticipated.

For now, though, they remained focused on their own journeys, unaware that the answers they sought might lie not just in the shadows of their histories, but in the light of shared humanity.

Chapter 4: The Unexpected Encounter

The next day, Vivaan found himself drawn to a quiet corner of Connaught Place—a stark contrast to the usual hustle and bustle of Delhi's commercial heart. He had taken the afternoon off from work, citing a vague "personal errand" to his manager. Truthfully, he needed space to think, to process the revelations from the journal and the lingering questions raised by the mysterious letter.

He wandered aimlessly through the labyrinthine alleys, past shops selling everything from antique trinkets to modern gadgets, until he stumbled upon a small, unassuming café tucked away behind a row of bustling storefronts. Its sign read "The Lantern's Glow" in faded gold letters, and something about it felt inviting—almost magnetic.

Inside, the café was dimly lit, with soft jazz playing in the background. The walls were adorned with vintage lanterns of all shapes and sizes, casting warm, flickering light across the room. Vivaan ordered a cup of masala chai and settled into a corner table, pulling out the journal once again. As he flipped through its pages, trying to piece together Radha's story, he didn't notice the man who approached him until a shadow fell across the table.

"May I join you?" the voice asked, low and gravelly, yet oddly soothing.

Vivaan looked up to see an elderly man standing before him. His silver hair was neatly combed, and his piercing gray eyes seemed to hold centuries of wisdom. He wore a simple kurta-pajama, but there was an air of quiet dignity about him that commanded respect.

"Of course," Vivaan said, gesturing to the empty chair across from him.

The man sat down, his gaze lingering on the journal in Vivaan's hands. "Family history, is it?" he asked, nodding toward the book. "Not many people take the time to look back these days."

Vivaan hesitated, unsure whether to share his story with a complete stranger. But there was something disarming about the man's presence—an aura of calm that put him at ease. "Yes," he admitted. "I'm trying to understand... well, myself, I suppose. And maybe my family too."

The man smiled faintly, as if he'd expected this answer. "Ah, the search for meaning. It's a journey we all undertake, though few dare to acknowledge it openly."

They sat in silence for a moment, the hum of conversation around them fading into the background. Then the man leaned forward slightly, his expression thoughtful. "You know, life is like a lantern. Its glow reveals only what lies beneath it, leaving much in shadow. But those shadows are not empty—they hold truths waiting to be uncovered."

Vivaan frowned, intrigued but uncertain. "What do you mean?"

The man gestured toward the journal. "Your ancestor, Radha. She left because she sought answers beyond the confines of her world. Her choice may have caused pain, but it also planted seeds of curiosity in those who came after her—including you."

Vivaan's heart skipped a beat. How could this stranger possibly know about Radha? Before he could ask, the man continued.

"Every life is connected, Mr. Gupta. The choices we make ripple outward, touching others in ways we cannot foresee. Sometimes,

understanding our past requires us to step into the unknown—
to embrace uncertainty and trust that the path will reveal itself."

Vivaan stared at him, stunned. "How do you know my name?"

The man chuckled softly, the sound almost musical. "Let's just
say I've been watching your journey unfold. You're not alone in
this quest, though it may feel that way at times."

Before Vivaan could press further, the man stood, his chair
scraping gently against the tiled floor. "Remember this: every
encounter has a purpose. Even ours." With that, he turned and
walked toward the door, disappearing into the crowd outside.

Vivaan sat frozen, his mind racing. Who was that man? And
what did he mean by "watching my journey"? The encounter left
him with more questions than answers, but one thing was
certain—the stranger's words had ignited a spark within him. If
Radha's story held the key to understanding his own, then he
owed it to himself—and perhaps to his family—to uncover the
truth.

As he packed up the journal and prepared to leave, Vivaan
noticed something on the table where the man had been sitting:
a small brass lantern, its flame flickering gently despite the
absence of wind. Beneath it lay a note written in elegant script:

"Shadows dance when light moves. Move boldly, Vivaan Gupta. The answers lie ahead."

Meanwhile, Saachi spent the evening reflecting on her father's legacy. After putting Atharv to bed, she pulled out an old diary he had given her years ago. Inside were notes he had jotted down during difficult times—words of encouragement meant to inspire her when life felt overwhelming. One entry caught her eye:

"When the road seems darkest, remember that even the smallest flame can guide you home."

Tears welled in her eyes as she realized how much strength she had drawn from his teachings without fully acknowledging it. Perhaps finding stability wasn't just about financial security—it was about reigniting the inner fire her father had nurtured in her.

In East Delhi, Bharat attended the storytelling event at the library, nervous but hopeful. As he listened to others share their stories, he felt a sense of kinship with the strangers around him.

When it was his turn, he spoke about Meera—the girl who had taught him that resilience could bloom even in the harshest conditions. By the end of his tale, several attendees approached him, thanking him for reminding them of the power of mentorship and connection.

One woman, in particular, lingered after the event. She introduced herself as Anjali, a former student of Bharat's whom he barely remembered. "You changed my life," she said simply, her eyes shining with gratitude. "I just wanted to thank you."

Bharat felt a lump rise in his throat. For the first time in months, he felt seen—not as a retired teacher, but as someone whose actions still mattered.

Unbeknownst to Vivaan, Saachi, and Bharat, their paths were growing closer, guided by forces they couldn't yet comprehend. Each of them carried a lantern, however faint, illuminating their individual journeys. Together, they would soon discover that the light of one could ignite the flames of many.

Chapter 5: The Journey Begins

The morning sun rose over Delhi, casting golden light across rooftops and awakening the city from its slumber. For Vivaan Gupta, it marked the beginning of a new chapter—not just in his external quest to uncover Radha's secrets, but in his internal journey to understand himself as part of something greater.

Sitting cross-legged on the balcony of his flat, Vivaan held the brass lantern the enigmatic stranger had left behind. Its flame flickered gently, unaffected by the breeze. He stared at it intently, recalling the man's words: "Shadows dance when light moves. Move boldly, Vivaan Gupta. The answers lie ahead."

What did it mean? How could he "move boldly" when so much of his life felt uncertain? Yet, as he gazed at the flame, an unexpected calm washed over him. There was something mesmerizing about its steady glow—a reminder that even the smallest light could dispel darkness.

For the first time, Vivaan allowed himself to entertain the possibility that there was more to life than what met the eye. Could it be true, as the stranger suggested, that every encounter had a purpose? That his search for meaning wasn't random, but part of a larger design?

He closed his eyes and focused on his breath, letting the sounds of the city fade into the background. In the stillness, he sensed a presence—an unseen force that seemed to hum Bharateath the surface of reality. It wasn't something he could explain logically; it simply was. And in that moment, he realized that perhaps the answers he sought weren't "out there" in documents or clues—they were already within him, waiting to be acknowledged.

When Unnati joined him a few minutes later, she found him smiling softly, a look of quiet determination in his eyes. "You seem... different," she said, studying him curiously.

"I think I am," Vivaan replied. "I'm not sure how to explain it yet, but I feel like I'm starting to see things differently."

Unnati didn't press further. Instead, she squeezed his hand reassuringly, trusting that whatever transformation was unfolding would reveal itself in time.

Across town, Saachi stood before her bedroom mirror, clutching the old diary her father had given her. She had spent hours poring over its pages the previous night, rediscovering the wisdom hidden within its worn covers. One phrase kept echoing in her mind: "Even the smallest flame can guide you home."

But what did "home" mean for her? Was it financial stability? A loving partner? Or something deeper—a sense of belonging to herself and the world around her?

As she dressed for the day, Saachi made a decision. She wouldn't let fear dictate her choices anymore. If her father had taught her anything, it was that resilience came from believing in possibilities—even when they seemed impossible. She resolved to take one step today, no matter how small, toward creating the life she envisioned for herself and Atharv.

Her first action? Signing up for a local entrepreneurship workshop aimed at helping single mothers start small businesses. As she filled out the registration form, a wave of excitement coursed through her. For the first time in years, she felt aligned with a higher purpose—as if the universe itself was conspiring to support her dreams.

In East Delhi, Bharat sat in his armchair, reflecting on the storytelling event and Anjali's heartfelt gratitude. Her words had stirred something deep within him—a realization that his impact extended far beyond the classroom walls. Though he had retired, his legacy lived on in the lives he had touched.

But what about his own life? What legacy did he wish to leave behind now?

Bharat closed his eyes and imagined himself as a thread in a vast tapestry, connected to countless others through invisible bonds of energy and intention. He thought about the students he had mentored, the lessons he had shared, and the love he had carried for his late wife. Each of these experiences was a ripple, contributing to the flow of existence.

A sudden clarity dawned on him: he wasn't done teaching. Not in the traditional sense, perhaps, but in a broader, more universal way. His role was to remind others—and himself—that we are all expressions of infinite intelligence, capable of tapping into the boundless potential within us.

With renewed purpose, Bharat decided to volunteer at a community center, offering free workshops on storytelling and personal growth. As he drafted an email to propose the idea, he felt a surge of joy. This wasn't just about filling his days—it was about aligning with the rhythm of life and allowing it to guide him forward.

Though Vivaan, Saachi, and Bharat remained unaware of each other's decisions, their actions were threads in the same cosmic web. Each of them was beginning to awaken to the truth that life is energy, frequency, and infinite intelligence. They were learning to trust the whispers of their hearts and believe in the reality already present within them.

And as they took these tentative steps, the universe responded—not with fanfare, but with subtle nudges and synchronicities that reaffirmed their connection to something greater. The journey ahead would test their courage and faith, but they were no longer walking blindly. They were moving boldly, guided by the light within.

Because everything already existed. All they had to do was believe.

Chapter 6: The Road Less Traveled

The journey toward self-discovery is rarely a straight path. For Vivaan, Saachi, and Bharat, the road ahead was fraught with challenges that tested their courage, faith, and determination. Yet, it was in these moments of struggle that they discovered their true strength—and the invisible threads connecting them to something greater.

Vivaan: Facing Obstacles and Discovering Cosmic Energy

Vivaan's newfound commitment to aligning with the flow of life didn't shield him from adversity. In fact, the universe seemed determined to test his resolve almost immediately. At work, tensions escalated when his multinational corporation announced plans for a major restructuring. Rumors swirled about layoffs, and Vivaan found himself under immense pressure to prove his value. His manager assigned him an overwhelming number of projects, each with impossible deadlines.

Initially, Vivaan reverted to his old habits—working late into the night, sacrificing sleep and family time, and drowning in stress. But one evening, as he sat slumped at his desk, staring blankly at spreadsheets, he felt a familiar whisper in his mind:

"You cannot solve problems with the same mindset that created them."

The words jolted him awake. He realized he was trying to tackle these challenges using fear-based thinking rather than trusting in the infinite intelligence within him. Determined to shift his perspective, Vivaan decided to take a break. He stepped onto the balcony of his office building, gazing out at the city lights below. Closing his eyes, he focused on his breath, allowing the chaos to fade away.

In that moment of stillness, he sensed the presence of the life force once again. Its voice was gentle yet firm:

"Resilience is not about enduring hardship; it is about flowing with it. Trust that every challenge carries a gift."

Vivaan returned to his desk with renewed clarity. Instead of panicking, he broke down each task into manageable steps and prioritized based on alignment with his values. When faced with a particularly daunting project, he reminded himself: This is an opportunity to grow. I have everything I need to succeed. To his amazement, solutions came effortlessly, and his colleagues marveled at his efficiency.

At home, Vivaan applied similar principles to strengthen his relationships. During a heated argument with Unnati about finances, he paused mid-sentence, recognizing the underlying fear driving her frustration. Instead of reacting defensively, he listened empathetically and offered reassurance. Their bond deepened as a result.

One day, while meditating, Vivaan received profound guidance about balancing life. The life force spoke to him:

"True abundance arises when you nurture your body, mind, and soul equally. Prioritize what truly matters, and let go of distractions."

Inspired, Vivaan restructured his schedule. He began each morning with meditation and journaling, setting intentions for the day. He allocated specific blocks of time for work, family, and personal growth, ensuring no single area dominated his life. By aligning his actions with his values, Vivaan experienced a sense of harmony he'd never known before.

Saachi: Overcoming Financial Struggles Through Faith

For Saachi, the road less traveled meant confronting her deepest fears about financial instability. Despite her growing success with the café snacks business, she often doubted whether she could provide enough for Atharv's future. One afternoon, as she balanced her accounts, panic gripped her heart. Expenses were piling up faster than expected, and she feared she wouldn't be able to keep up.

Desperate for guidance, Saachi turned to the diary her father had given her. Flipping through its pages, she stumbled upon an entry that resonated deeply:

"Faith is the bridge between where you are and where you want to be. Believe in the unseen, and it will manifest."

Saachi closed her eyes and visualized herself achieving financial stability—not just for survival but for thriving. She imagined Atharv attending a prestigious school, their home filled with laughter, and her business flourishing. Though skeptical, she repeated affirmations daily:

- I am capable of creating abundance.

- Every challenge brings me closer to my dreams.

To her astonishment, opportunities began presenting themselves unexpectedly. A local entrepreneur approached her about collaborating on a larger-scale catering venture, offering resources and mentorship. Encouraged by this synchronicity, Saachi embraced the belief that the universe supported her efforts.

Through meditation, Saachi also learned to release anxiety about the future. She practiced gratitude, focusing on the blessings already present in her life. Slowly but surely, her mindset shifted from scarcity to abundance.

Bharat: Rediscovering Purpose Through Perseverance

Bharat's journey was marked by moments of doubt and uncertainty. After volunteering at the community center, he initially struggled to connect with participants. Some dismissed his workshops as outdated, while others questioned the relevance of storytelling in today's fast-paced world. Discouraged, Bharat considered giving up.

But then, during a quiet evening at home, he recalled Anjali's heartfelt gratitude. Her words echoed in his mind: "You changed my life." Inspired, Bharat resolved to persevere. He adapted his approach, incorporating modern storytelling techniques and interactive exercises to engage younger audiences. Gradually, attendance increased, and feedback became overwhelmingly positive.

One participant—a young woman named Priya—shared how Bharat's workshop helped her overcome stage fright and pursue her dream of becoming a public speaker. Touched by her story, Bharat realized that his purpose extended beyond teaching; it was about empowering others to express their unique gifts.

Through meditation, Bharat discovered the importance of surrendering control. He learned to trust that his contributions, however small, rippled outward in ways he couldn't always see. This realization brought him peace and fulfillment.

Serendipity: Guiding Them Forward

As Vivaan, Saachi, and Bharat navigated their respective challenges, moments of serendipity illuminated their paths. For Vivaan, it was meeting an old colleague who introduced him to a mindfulness coach, further deepening his understanding of meditation. For Saachi, it was stumbling upon a free online course about entrepreneurship, which equipped her with valuable skills. And for Bharat, it was reconnecting with Meera— the former student whose story had stayed with him for years.

She revealed that she now worked as a counselor, helping children in shelters find hope and purpose.

These coincidences reinforced their belief in the interconnectedness of all things. They began to see life not as a series of random events but as a divine orchestration designed to awaken humanity to its highest potential.

Chapter 7: The Mirror of Self-Discovery

Acknowledged its presence and thanked it for trying to shield him from harm. Then, he spoke firmly but kindly:

"I understand your fears, but I no longer need you to control me. I am learning to trust myself and the infinite intelligence that guides me. Together, we can let go of these old patterns."

As Vivaan extended this olive branch to his inner critic, he felt a weight lift from his chest. The shadowy figure began to dissolve, replaced by a warm glow that filled his entire being. It was as if he had finally made peace with the parts of himself, he once despised.

This breakthrough wasn't just emotional—it manifested in tangible ways. At work, Vivaan stopped second-guessing his decisions and started trusting his instincts. When a high-stakes project arose, he approached it not with anxiety but with confidence, knowing that he was capable of handling whatever came his way. His colleagues noticed the change; one even remarked, "You seem unstoppable lately."

At home, Vivaan's newfound self-acceptance deepened his relationships. He confessed to Unnati some of the insecurities he'd kept hidden for years, expecting judgment. Instead, she held his hand and said, "Vivaan, you've always been enough—for me, for Shanaya, for everyone who loves you. You just needed to see it for yourself."

Saachi: Releasing Guilt and Embracing Strength

For Saachi, the mirror of self-discovery revealed a different kind of shadow: guilt. She carried the heavy burden of believing she hadn't done enough for Atharv after her husband left. Every missed school event, every late-night shift, every moment she couldn't give him her full attention weighed on her conscience. Though she worked tirelessly to provide for him, she often felt like a failure as a mother.

One afternoon, while preparing snacks for her growing catering business, Saachi found herself staring at her reflection in the stainless steel counter. Her eyes were tired, her shoulders slumped under the weight of unspoken regrets. Suddenly, she remembered something her father used to say:

"The strongest trees grow roots deep enough to hold their branches steady."

Inspired, Saachi decided to confront her guilt head-on. That evening, she sat down with Atharv and shared her feelings openly. "Beta," she began hesitantly, "I want you to know how much I love you. Sometimes I worry I haven't been the best mom because I've had to work so hard. But I'm doing my best, and I hope you can forgive me for the times I wasn't there."

To her astonishment, Atharv threw his arms around her and said, "Mama, you're the best mom ever. You work so hard for us, and I'm proud of you."

Tears streamed down Saachi's face as she hugged him tightly. In that moment, she realized that her guilt stemmed not from reality but from her own unrealistic expectations. She had been judging herself against an impossible standard—one shaped by society's demands rather than her son's needs.

Through meditation, Saachi learned to release this guilt and embrace her strength. She visualized herself as a tree, its roots digging deep into the earth, drawing nourishment from the soil of resilience and love. With each breath, she affirmed:

"I am strong. I am capable. I am enough."

This shift transformed her approach to life. She began setting boundaries at work, ensuring she had time for Atharv without sacrificing her ambitions. Her business flourished, not because she worked harder but because she worked smarter—and with joy.

Bharat: Letting Go of Grief and Finding Purpose

For Bharat, the mirror of self-discovery brought him face-to-face with grief—the loss of his wife and the loneliness that followed. Though he had thrown himself into volunteering and mentoring, a part of him still felt empty, as if he were living half a life.

One night, unable to sleep, Bharat wandered into his study and pulled out an old photo album. Flipping through the pages, he came across a picture of his wife smiling brightly, her arm wrapped around his shoulder. Memories flooded back—their laughter-filled evenings, their quiet mornings over tea, the way she always knew how to calm his worries.

Bharat allowed himself to cry, releasing years of pent-up sorrow. As the tears subsided, he whispered, "I miss you so much. But I know you'd want me to keep going—to live fully."

In that moment, Bharat understood that grief wasn't something to overcome but something to integrate. His wife's love hadn't disappeared; it lived on in the lessons she taught him, the memories they shared, and the legacy he continued to build.

Through storytelling, Bharat found a way to honor her memory. He began weaving anecdotes about her into his workshops, sharing how her wisdom had shaped his life. Participants responded deeply, inspired by his vulnerability and authenticity. One woman approached him after a session and said, "Your stories remind me that love never truly leaves us. Thank you for sharing your heart."

Bharat realized that his purpose wasn't just to teach others—it was to heal himself through connection. By embracing his grief, he discovered a renewed sense of meaning and belonging.

Symbolism: The Light Within the Shadows

Each character's journey of self-discovery was marked by powerful symbols that represented their growth. For Vivaan, it was the image of a lantern—a reminder that even the smallest flame could dispel darkness. For Saachi, it was the tree, symbolizing strength rooted in resilience. And for Bharat, it was the photograph, embodying the enduring power of love.

These symbols served as anchors, grounding them in moments of doubt and reminding them of their inherent worth. They learned that self-acceptance wasn't about erasing imperfections but about embracing the entirety of who they were—flaws and all.

By the end of this chapter, Vivaan, Saachi, and Bharat stand transformed, having confronted their inner demons and emerged stronger. Each has taken a monumental step toward self-acceptance, recognizing that true growth begins with loving oneself unconditionally. Though their paths remain distinct, the threads connecting them grow tighter, hinting at the profound revelations yet to come.

Chapter 8: The Bonds We Forge

As Vivaan, Saachi, and Bharat continued along their respective paths of self-discovery, they began to notice subtle shifts—not just within themselves but in the world around them. It was as if the universe had conspired to bring them closer together, weaving their lives into an intricate tapestry of connection. Though they remained unaware of each other's existence for now, their actions rippled outward, touching others in ways that would soon reveal profound synchronicities.

.

Vivaan: Strengthening Family Ties Through Vulnerability

Vivaan's newfound self-acceptance transformed not only his relationship with himself but also with his family. One evening, during dinner, he decided to share more openly about his spiritual journey. He told Unnati and Shanaya about the mysterious letter, the enigmatic stranger, and the life force he had encountered through meditation. At first, Unnati listened skeptically, her brow furrowed in thought. But as Vivaan spoke with genuine conviction, she softened, realizing how much this journey meant to him.

"Papa, does that mean you talk to God?" Shanaya asked, her wide eyes sparkling with curiosity.

Vivaan chuckled softly. "In a way, yes. But it's not just one god—it's like... everything is connected. Like we're all part of something bigger."

Shanaya tilted her head, pondering this idea. Then she grinned. "So I'm part of the big thing too?"

"Yes, beta," Vivaan replied, smiling warmly. "You're a very important part."

This conversation marked a turning point in their household. Vivaan's willingness to be vulnerable inspired Unnati to open up about her own struggles—her fears of inadequacy as a homemaker and her longing for creative fulfillment. Together, they brainstormed ways for her to pursue her passion for painting, which she had set aside years ago. By supporting each other's dreams, they created a home filled with love, encouragement, and mutual respect.

Even Shanaya noticed the change. "Our house feels happier now," she declared one night as they sat together watching the stars from their balcony. "Like magic."

Vivaan smiled, knowing she was right. Their bond had deepened because they had chosen to face their shadows together, emerging stronger as a unit.

Saachi: Building a Support Network Through Shared Struggles

For Saachi, the bonds she forged became a lifeline during challenging times. As her catering business grew, so did the demands on her time and energy. There were days when exhaustion threatened to overwhelm her, leaving her questioning whether she could keep going. But instead of retreating into isolation, Saachi leaned on the community she had built—the women from the entrepreneurship workshop who had become her closest friends.

One afternoon, after a particularly grueling day, Saachi met with her friend Rekha at a local café. Over steaming cups of chai, she confessed her fears: "What if I fail? What if I can't provide for Atharv?"

Rekha placed a reassuring hand on hers. "Saachi, look how far you've come already. You didn't start this business to prove anything to anyone—you did it because it's your dream. Trust yourself. We're here for you, no matter what."

Her words struck a chord. Saachi realized that success wasn't measured by external achievements but by the strength of the connections she nurtured along the way. Inspired, she organized a monthly gathering for fellow entrepreneurs to share their experiences, challenges, and triumphs. These meetings became a source of inspiration and accountability, reminding everyone that they weren't alone in their struggles.

Through these interactions, Saachi discovered the power of collective energy. When she visualized her goals, she imagined not just herself succeeding but her entire community thriving alongside her. This mindset shift brought unexpected blessings—a new client referred by a friend, a mentor offering guidance, and even Atharv expressing pride in her accomplishments.

"You're my hero, Mama," he said one evening as they prepared dinner together. "You make me believe I can do anything."

Tears welled in Saachi's eyes as she hugged him tightly. She knew then that her efforts weren't just about providing for her son—they were about showing him the value of resilience, courage, and connection.

Bharat: Finding Belonging Through Service

Bharat's journey toward deeper connections unfolded through his work at the community center. Initially, he saw his role as purely instructional—sharing stories and teaching skills. But over time, he realized that his impact extended far beyond the classroom. Participants began confiding in him, sharing their hopes, fears, and dreams. Through listening with empathy, Bharat discovered that his presence alone was a gift—a reminder that everyone has a story worth telling.

One participant, a young man named Arjun, stood out to Bharat. Arjun struggled with anxiety and often doubted his ability to succeed. During a storytelling session, Bharat encouraged him to share a personal experience—a moment of overcoming adversity. Though hesitant at first, Arjun eventually recounted how he had helped his younger sister navigate bullying at school. The room erupted in applause, and Arjun's face lit up with pride.

Afterward, Arjun approached Bharat and said, "Thank you for believing in me. No one has ever done that before."

Bharat felt a lump rise in his throat. "You have so much potential, Arjun. Don't let fear hold you back."

Their interaction reminded Bharat of Meera—the former student whose resilience had inspired him decades ago. He realized that his purpose wasn't just to teach but to empower others to see their own worth. By fostering a sense of belonging, he created a space where people felt seen, heard, and valued.

In turn, Bharat found solace in these connections. The loneliness that had haunted him since his wife's passing began to fade, replaced by a renewed sense of purpose. He understood now that grief didn't isolate him—it connected him to others who carried their own burdens. By sharing his story, he invited others to do the same, creating a cycle of healing and growth.

Interconnectedness: Threads Woven Together

Though Vivaan, Saachi, and Bharat remained unaware of each other's existence, their lives intertwined in subtle yet meaningful ways. For instance, one of Saachi's catering clients turned out to be a colleague of Vivaan's, who praised her dedication and creativity during lunch breaks. Meanwhile, Bharat's workshops attracted participants who worked at the same multinational corporation as Vivaan, spreading ripples of positivity throughout the organization.

These invisible threads hinted at a larger truth: none of them were truly alone. Their individual acts of courage and faith contributed to a collective energy that uplifted those around them. Whether through family, friendship, or service, they were learning that connection was the key to unlocking true abundance.

By the end of this chapter, Vivaan, Saachi, and Bharat stand united—not physically, but spiritually—through the bonds they've forged. Each has discovered that personal growth isn't a solitary endeavor; it's a shared journey fueled by love, support, and the recognition that we are all part of the same universal tapestry.

Chapter 9: The Heart of the Matter

Love is the thread that binds humanity together—a force so powerful it can heal wounds, transcend barriers, and illuminate even the darkest corners of existence. For Vivaan, Saachi, and Bharat, this truth became undeniable as they navigated pivotal moments in their lives. Through acts of love—both given and received—they discovered deeper layers of themselves and the world around them.

Vivaan: Rediscovering Love Within Family

For Vivaan, the heart of the matter lay in redefining his understanding of familial love. Growing up, he had equated love with duty—providing for his family, meeting societal expectations, and ensuring everyone's needs were met. But as he embraced his spiritual journey, he began to see love not as an obligation but as a choice—an act of presence, attentiveness, and unconditional acceptance.

One evening, during a rare weekend when the entire extended family gathered at his parents' home in North Delhi, Vivaan found himself reflecting on the dynamics between him, his brothers Kiaan and Ditya, and their parents, R.K. and Mannat Gupta. For years, he had felt overshadowed by his siblings' achievements, believing he didn't measure up to their success. Yet, sitting beside his father as they sipped tea on the veranda, Vivaan noticed something he'd never seen before: pride in R.K.'s eyes.

"You've always been the glue that holds us together," R.K. said softly, breaking the comfortable silence. "Your kindness, your patience—it's what makes our family strong."

Vivaan was taken aback. He had spent so much time doubting his worth that he hadn't realized others saw him differently. In that moment, he understood that love wasn't about comparison or competition; it was about contribution—the unique gifts each person brought to the table.

This realization deepened his bond with Unnati and Shanaya as well. One night, after tucking Shanaya into bed, Vivaan sat with Unnati on the balcony, gazing at the stars. They spoke openly about their dreams—not just for themselves but for their family. Unnati confessed her longing to return to painting, while Vivaan shared his vision of writing a book about his spiritual journey. Together, they made a pact to support each other's aspirations without fear or judgment.

"I love you more than words can say," Unnati whispered, resting her head on his shoulder. "Not because of what you do, but because of who you are."

Tears welled in Vivaan's eyes as he held her close. He realized then that love wasn't confined to grand gestures or material achievements—it thrived in the quiet, everyday moments of connection.

Saachi: Embracing Love Through Sacrifice and Growth

For Saachi, love took the form of sacrifice and resilience. As a single mother, she had poured every ounce of her energy into raising Atharv, often neglecting her own needs in the process. While her dedication stemmed from love, it sometimes left her feeling depleted and unseen. But through her growing business and friendships, Saachi began to understand that love also required balance—a mutual exchange of care and support.

One afternoon, as she prepared orders for a large catering event, Saachi felt overwhelmed by the sheer volume of work. Just as she was about to give up, her friend Rekha arrived unannounced, bringing along two other women from their entrepreneurship group. "We're here to help," Rekha declared firmly. "You've done so much for us—it's our turn to step up."

Overwhelmed with gratitude, Saachi allowed herself to lean on them, delegating tasks and sharing responsibilities. Together, they completed the order ahead of schedule, laughing and bonding over shared struggles. That evening, as they celebrated their success with cups of chai, Saachi felt a profound sense of belonging.

"You remind me of my mom," one of the women, Priya, said suddenly. "She worked just as hard to provide for us. Seeing you fight for Atharv inspires me to honor her memory."

Saachi's heart swelled with emotion. She realized that love wasn't limited to blood ties—it extended to the connections we forge with those who walk alongside us. By opening herself to receive help, she had created space for others to express their love in return.

Later that week, Atharv surprised her with a handmade card that read: "To the best mom ever. Thank you for everything." Tears streamed down Saachi's face as she hugged him tightly. In that moment, she understood that love wasn't about perfection—it was about showing up, day after day, with an open heart.

And for Bharat, love became a bittersweet reminder of life's fragility and beauty. Though his wife had passed away years ago, her presence lingered in every corner of his life—from the photographs on his walls to the recipes he still cooked from memory. For a long time, Bharat had avoided forming new connections, fearing that doing so would diminish her memory. But through his work at the community center, he began to see love not as a finite resource but as an infinite expression of the universe.

One evening, during a storytelling session, a participant named Anjali shared a poignant tale about losing her partner and finding solace in helping others. Her words resonated deeply with Bharat, prompting him to open up about his own grief. Afterward, Anjali approached him and said, "Your wife must have been an incredible woman. But I think she'd want you to keep loving—to let people into your heart again."

Bharat nodded, tears glistening in his eyes. He realized that honoring his wife's memory didn't mean closing himself off; it meant continuing to spread the love she had taught him. Over time, he formed meaningful friendships with participants like Arjun and Anjali, finding joy in their laughter and comfort in their shared experiences.

Through these connections, Bharat learned that love transcends physical presence—it lives on in the impact we leave behind. Whether through mentoring, volunteering, or simply listening, he understood that every act of kindness was a reflection of the love he carried within.

Lessons in Love: Joy and Loss

As Vivaan, Saachi, and Bharat explored the multifaceted nature of love, they encountered both its joys and its losses. For Vivaan, it was the realization that love begins with self-acceptance and extends outward to touch every relationship. For Saachi, it was the understanding that love requires vulnerability—not just giving but receiving. And for Bharat, it was the acceptance that love endures beyond death, shaping the legacy we leave behind.

Each of them came to see love not as a fleeting emotion but as a universal force that connects all beings. It was in love that they found strength, purpose, and healing—and it was through love that they continued to grow.

Chapter 10: The Quest for Happiness

Happiness is a paradox—it often eludes those who chase it relentlessly, yet reveals itself effortlessly to those who stop searching. For Vivaan, Saachi, and Bharat, the quest for happiness became less about attaining something outside themselves and more about recognizing the abundance already present within their lives. Through moments of stillness, reflection, and shared joy, they discovered that true happiness resides in the simplicity of being.

Vivaan: Finding Joy in Presence

For Vivaan, happiness had long been equated with success—promotions at work, societal approval, and meeting expectations. But as he delved deeper into his spiritual journey, he began to question whether these external markers truly brought fulfillment. One morning, during meditation, he visualized himself standing at a crossroads, each path representing a different pursuit: wealth, recognition, family, and inner peace. To his surprise, his heart gravitated toward the last option—a quiet, unassuming path bathed in soft light.

That day, Vivaan made a conscious decision to prioritize presence over productivity. At work, instead of rushing through meetings and emails, he took time to engage meaningfully with colleagues. He noticed how a simple compliment or moment of genuine connection could brighten someone's day—including his own. At home, he savored meals with Unnati and Shanaya, listening intently to their stories rather than letting his mind wander to unfinished tasks.

One evening, as they sat together on the balcony watching the sunset, Shanaya turned to him and asked, "Papa, are you happy?"

Vivaan paused, considering the question deeply. Then he smiled and replied, "Yes, beta. Right now, I am."

It wasn't the kind of happiness that came from achieving a goal or acquiring something new. It was quieter, subtler—a sense of contentment rooted in the present moment. Vivaan realized that happiness wasn't a destination; it was a state of being, available whenever he chose to embrace it.

Saachi: Discovering Abundance in Simplicity

For Saachi, the quest for happiness had always been intertwined with financial stability. As a single mother, she believed that providing for Atharv meant securing a comfortable future—one free from worry and scarcity. Yet, as her catering business flourished, she noticed that money alone didn't fill the void inside her. There were days when she felt overwhelmed by responsibilities, despite having more resources than ever before.

One afternoon, while delivering an order to a client's home, Saachi stumbled upon a small park tucked away behind rows of bustling shops. Intrigued, she decided to take a break and sit beneath a sprawling neem tree. The air was cool, and the sound of children playing nearby brought a smile to her face. She closed her eyes and breathed deeply, feeling a sense of calm wash over her.

In that moment, Saachi understood that happiness wasn't tied to external circumstances—it was cultivated internally. She thought about the mornings she spent cooking breakfast for Atharv, the laughter they shared during movie nights, and the pride she felt when customers praised her food. These moments, though seemingly ordinary, were rich with meaning.

Inspired, Saachi began practicing gratitude daily. Each night before bed, she wrote down three things she appreciated about her life—whether it was a kind word from a friend, a beautiful sunrise, or simply the warmth of her son's hug. Over time, this practice shifted her perspective, helping her see abundance in places she had once overlooked.

"Mama, why do you look so peaceful lately?" Atharv asked one evening as they prepared dinner together.

Saachi smiled, ruffling his hair affectionately. "Because I've learned that happiness doesn't come from having more—it comes from appreciating what we already have."

Bharat: Embracing Joy in Connection

For Bharat, happiness had become elusive after his wife's passing. Though he found purpose in mentoring others, there were moments when loneliness crept in, leaving him yearning for companionship. Yet, through his interactions at the community center, he began to rediscover the joy of human connection.

One evening, during a storytelling session, a participant named Anjali shared a humorous anecdote about misplacing her glasses only to find them perched atop her head. The room erupted in laughter, and Bharat found himself chuckling along, tears streaming down his face. It was a rare moment of pure, unguarded joy—one that reminded him of the lighthearted conversations he used to share with his wife.

Afterward, Anjali approached him and said, "Your laugh is contagious, Mr. Mathur. Thank you for sharing it with us."

Bharat felt a warmth spread through his chest. He realized that happiness didn't require grand gestures or dramatic events—it could be found in the simplest acts of connection. Whether it was sharing a joke, offering a listening ear, or enjoying a cup of chai with friends, these moments added color to his life.

Encouraged by this insight, Bharat began seeking out opportunities for joy. He joined a local book club, rekindling his love for literature, and started volunteering at a senior citizens' center, where he formed meaningful friendships with residents. Through these experiences, he learned that happiness wasn't about avoiding pain or loss—it was about embracing life fully, with all its ups and downs.

Contrasting Societal Expectations with Personal Fulfillment

As Vivaan, Saachi, and Bharat reflected on their journeys, they recognized a common theme: societal expectations often clashed with personal fulfillment. Society measured success in terms of wealth, status, and achievement, yet true happiness stemmed from authenticity, simplicity, and connection.

For Vivaan, this realization meant rejecting the pressure to conform to high-class norms in Pitampura. Instead, he embraced his values of generosity and kindness, finding joy in relationships rather than material possessions. For Saachi, it meant letting go of the belief that financial security alone could bring happiness. By focusing on gratitude and presence, she discovered abundance in everyday moments. And for Bharat, it meant stepping out of isolation and allowing himself to form new connections, proving that love and joy endure beyond loss.

Each of them came to understand that happiness is a choice—a decision to focus on what truly matters rather than chasing illusions of perfection.

By the end of this chapter, Vivaan, Saachi, and Bharat stand united—not physically, but spiritually—through their shared understanding of happiness. They have learned that joy isn't something to seek externally; it is already within them, waiting to be acknowledged and cherished.

Chapter 11: The Secrets of the Universe

The universe is a vast, intricate web of energy, frequency, and infinite intelligence—a cosmic dance that invites humanity to participate in its unfolding mystery. For Vivaan, Saachi, and Bharat, this truth became undeniable as they encountered moments that challenged their understanding of existence and purpose. Guided by wisdom from unexpected sources, they began to see themselves not as isolated individuals but as integral parts of a greater whole.

Vivaan: Encountering the Cosmic Teacher

One evening, after a particularly enlightening meditation session, Vivaan felt an overwhelming urge to visit the same café where he had met the enigmatic stranger weeks earlier—"The Lantern's Glow." Though he hadn't planned to go there, something within him whispered that it was time.

As he entered the dimly lit space, he noticed an elderly man sitting in the corner, surrounded by stacks of books and papers. His presence radiated calm and authority, drawing Vivaan toward him like a magnet. The man looked up and smiled knowingly, as if he'd been expecting him.

"Welcome back, Vivaan Gupta," the man said softly, gesturing for him to sit. "I've been watching your journey unfold."

Vivaan hesitated, unsure whether to trust this stranger. But there was something disarming about his demeanor—an aura of wisdom that put him at ease. "Who are you?" he asked finally.

"I am merely a guide," the man replied. "Call me Anish. My role is to help seekers like yourself uncover the secrets of the universe."

Over the next hour, Anish shared insights that would forever alter Vivaan's perception of reality. He explained that everything in existence—people, objects, thoughts, emotions—is composed of energy vibrating at different frequencies. What humans perceive as "solid" or "real" is simply a manifestation of these vibrations.

"The key to mastering life lies in aligning your energy with the universal flow," Anish continued. "When you resist this flow, you create suffering. When you surrender to it, you experience harmony."

He introduced Vivaan to the concept of belief systems—the subconscious filters through which people interpret reality. "Your thoughts shape your world," Anish said. "If you believe scarcity exists, you will attract scarcity. If you believe abundance surrounds you, you will manifest abundance."

To illustrate this point, Anish handed Vivaan a small crystal pendant. "Carry this with you as a reminder of your connection to the infinite intelligence. Whenever doubt arises, hold it and feel the truth of who you are."

By the end of their conversation, Vivaan's mind buzzed with possibilities. He realized that the answers he sought weren't "out there"; they were within him, waiting to be acknowledged.

Saachi: Discovering Universal Laws Through Experience

For Saachi, the secrets of the universe revealed themselves not through words but through lived experience. One afternoon, while preparing snacks for a large catering order, she found herself overwhelmed by self-doubt. Despite her growing success, she worried that she wasn't good enough—that her efforts would never amount to anything meaningful.

Just as frustration threatened to consume her, a customer arrived to pick up their order. It was Rekha, one of her closest friends from the entrepreneurship group. Sensing Saachi's distress, Rekha sat down beside her and said gently, "Tell me what's bothering you."

Saachi poured out her fears, confessing that she often felt like an imposter despite her achievements. Rekha listened patiently, then shared a story about her own struggles with confidence. "What helped me," she said, "was realizing that we're all part of something bigger. Our successes aren't just ours—they belong to everyone who supports us."

Inspired, Saachi began exploring the idea of universal laws—the principles governing creation, such as cause and effect, vibration, and attraction. She learned that every action, thought, and emotion contributes to the collective energy field, influencing outcomes in ways both seen and unseen.

Through journaling and visualization, Saachi practiced aligning her intentions with these laws. Each morning, she affirmed:

- I am worthy of love and success.

- Every challenge brings me closer to my dreams.

- The universe conspires in my favor.

To her astonishment, opportunities began presenting themselves unexpectedly. A local café owner offered her a permanent spot to sell her snacks, and a food blogger featured her business online, bringing in new customers. Saachi realized that her belief in abundance had shifted her reality, proving that the universe responds to the energy we emit.

Bharat: Reflecting on Existence Through Storytelling

For Bharat, the secrets of the universe emerged through storytelling—a medium that allowed him to explore profound questions about life and purpose. During one workshop, a participant named Priya shared a tale about losing her job and discovering a passion for photography. Her courage inspired Bharat to reflect on his own journey.

That evening, as he prepared for bed, Bharat opened a journal and began writing his thoughts. He pondered the nature of existence, asking himself:

- Why are we here?

- What is the purpose of suffering?

- How can we find meaning in chaos?

As he wrote, fragments of answers surfaced—insights gleaned from years of teaching, mentoring, and living. He realized that life itself is the ultimate teacher, offering lessons through joy, pain, and everything in between. By embracing uncertainty and trusting the process, humans align themselves with the universe's creative power.

Encouraged by this realization, Bharat decided to incorporate philosophical discussions into his workshops. He introduced participants to concepts like interconnectedness, synchronicity, and the law of attraction, encouraging them to question their assumptions about reality. Together, they explored how thoughts, emotions, and actions ripple outward, shaping individual and collective experiences.

One participant, Arjun, approached Bharat afterward and said, "Thank you for helping me see that I'm not alone. We're all connected, aren't we?"

Bharat nodded, feeling a deep sense of fulfillment. He understood now that his purpose wasn't just to teach stories—it was to inspire others to write their own.

Pondering Life's Mysteries

As Vivaan, Saachi, and Bharat delved deeper into the secrets of the universe, they encountered questions that defied easy answers. Yet, rather than seeking definitive solutions, they embraced the mystery, recognizing that life's beauty lies in its complexity.

For Vivaan, this meant trusting in the infinite intelligence and allowing it to guide his path. For Saachi, it meant practicing gratitude and aligning her energy with universal laws. And for Bharat, it meant fostering curiosity and encouraging others to explore their own truths.

Each of them came to understand that the universe is not a puzzle to solve but a symphony to experience—a divine expression of love, creativity, and possibility.

Chapter 12: The Turning Point

Life has a way of testing us when we least expect it—pushing us to our limits and forcing us to confront the parts of ourselves we'd rather ignore. For Vivaan, Saachi, and Bharat, this chapter marked a turning point in their journeys. Each faced a crisis that shook them to their core, challenging their beliefs, exposing their vulnerabilities, and ultimately leading them to embrace authenticity as their greatest strength.

Vivaan: Facing Professional Turmoil with Courage

For Vivaan, the turning point came unexpectedly at work. After months of excelling in his role, he found himself embroiled in a corporate scandal involving allegations of financial misconduct within his department. Though Vivaan had no involvement in the wrongdoing, the investigation cast a shadow over his integrity, leaving him feeling betrayed and powerless.

The pressure mounted as colleagues distanced themselves, fearing guilt by association. Even some family members questioned whether he had been complicit, despite knowing his character. One evening, after a particularly grueling day of interrogations and accusations, Vivaan returned home drained and defeated. Sitting alone on the balcony, he stared at the city lights below, wondering if he had made a mistake pursuing a career that seemed so disconnected from his values.

Unnati joined him a few minutes later, placing a comforting hand on his shoulder. "You've always been honest and hardworking," she said softly. "Don't let others' doubts make you question yourself."

Her words struck a chord. Vivaan realized that the real challenge wasn't proving his innocence—it was staying true to his authentic self amidst chaos. He remembered Anish's teachings about aligning with universal energy and trusting in the flow of life. Taking a deep breath, he resolved to face the situation with transparency and grace.

Over the next few days, Vivaan cooperated fully with investigators, providing clear documentation of his actions. He also addressed his team openly, acknowledging the uncertainty while reaffirming his commitment to ethical practices. To his surprise, his honesty earned the respect of both colleagues and superiors. When the investigation concluded, it was revealed that Vivaan had indeed played no part in the misconduct. His reputation emerged stronger than ever, not because he fought back but because he chose authenticity over defensiveness.

Through this experience, Vivaan learned that vulnerability isn't a weakness—it's a source of power. By embracing his truth, he inspired others to do the same.

Saachi: Overcoming Self-Doubt Amidst Failure

For Saachi, the turning point arrived in the form of a devastating setback. A major catering order for a high-profile event went awry when a supplier failed to deliver key ingredients on time. Despite her best efforts to salvage the situation, the client was furious, threatening to sue and tarnish her fledgling business's reputation.

The incident left Saachi reeling with self-doubt. She questioned whether she was cut out for entrepreneurship, fearing that one misstep could undo all her hard work. That night, as she sat alone in her kitchen surrounded by uneaten snacks, tears streamed down her face. "Maybe I'm not good enough," she whispered to herself.

But then Atharv walked in, holding a drawing he had made earlier that day. It depicted Saachi standing tall, surrounded by smiling customers. "Mama, you're my hero," he said simply. "Don't give up."

His words reignited something within her—a spark of resilience she hadn't realized still burned. Determined to turn the situation around, Saachi reached out to the client and offered a heartfelt apology, along with a refund and a promise to rectify the mistake. To her relief, the client accepted her gesture, impressed by her accountability and sincerity.

Reflecting on the incident, Saachi recognized that failure wasn't the end—it was an opportunity to grow. She began implementing stricter quality checks and building stronger relationships with suppliers, ensuring such mistakes wouldn't happen again. More importantly, she embraced her imperfections, understanding that authenticity builds trust far more effectively than perfection.

"Sometimes falling is just part of flying," she wrote in her journal that night. "And I'm ready to soar again."

Bharat: Confronting Loneliness Through Vulnerability

For Bharat, the turning point stemmed from a deeply personal place—his lingering loneliness. Despite forming meaningful connections through his workshops, there were nights when the absence of his wife felt unbearable. He often wondered whether he would ever find companionship again or if he was destined to live out his days alone.

One evening, during a storytelling session, a participant named Anjali shared a poignant tale about losing her partner and finding solace in helping others. Her vulnerability resonated deeply with Bharat, prompting him to open up about his own grief. Afterward, Anjali approached him and said, "Your honesty touched me, Mr. Mathur. Thank you for sharing your heart."

Her kindness reminded Bharat that vulnerability creates bridges between people, fostering deeper connections. Inspired, he decided to step out of his comfort zone and attend social gatherings organized by friends and acquaintances. At first, he felt awkward and out of place, but gradually, he began to enjoy the camaraderie and laughter.

Through these interactions, Bharat discovered that loneliness wasn't a permanent state—it was a signal to reach out, to connect, to remind himself that love exists in many forms. Whether through friendships, mentorship, or even fleeting moments of shared joy, he realized that he was never truly alone.

"I don't need to fill the void," he wrote in his journal. "I just need to honor it—and let it guide me toward connection."

Vulnerability as Strength: The Power of Authenticity

As Vivaan, Saachi, and Bharat navigated their respective crises, they came to understand a universal truth: vulnerability is not a flaw—it is a gateway to transformation. By confronting their fears and insecurities head-on, they uncovered reservoirs of strength they hadn't known existed.

For Vivaan, authenticity meant standing firm in his values, even when others doubted him. For Saachi, it meant owning her mistakes and using them as stepping stones to success. And for Bharat, it meant allowing himself to be seen, creating space for new relationships to blossom.

Each of them emerged from their trials stronger, wiser, and more aligned with their true selves. They learned that authenticity doesn't shield us from pain—but it equips us to face it with courage and grace.

Chapter 13: The Light in the Darkness

In life's darkest moments, when despair threatens to consume us, it is often the smallest glimmers of hope that illuminate the path forward. For Vivaan, Saachi, and Bharat, this chapter became a testament to the resilience of the human spirit—the ability to rise above adversity and find beauty in the brokenness. Through acts of kindness, serendipitous encounters, and inner awakenings, they discovered that even in the depths of darkness, light persists.

Vivaan: A Stranger's Kindness Restores Faith

After the corporate scandal had been resolved, Vivaan returned to work with renewed determination. Yet, the emotional toll lingered. Though his colleagues treated him with respect, he couldn't shake the feeling of being judged—of carrying an invisible scar that others might never fully understand. Some nights, as he lay awake staring at the ceiling, he questioned whether he belonged in a world that valued appearances over authenticity.

One evening, while walking home from the office, Vivaan stopped at a small roadside stall to buy chai. As he waited for his order, he noticed an elderly man sitting nearby, sketching scenes of the bustling street on a weathered notepad. Intrigued, Vivaan struck up a conversation.

"I used to draw when I was younger," Vivaan admitted. "But life got in the way."

The man smiled warmly. "Life always gets in the way. But art reminds us why we're here—to create, to connect, to leave something behind."

His words resonated deeply with Vivaan. He realized that his journey wasn't just about surviving challenges—it was about creating meaning, even in the face of uncertainty. Inspired, he decided to revisit a long-forgotten hobby: painting. That weekend, he purchased supplies and set up a makeshift studio in the storeroom of his flat.

As he dipped his brush into vibrant colors, Vivaan felt a sense of peace wash over him. Each stroke became an expression of his emotions—his fears, his hopes, his dreams. When Unnati and Shanaya saw his first completed piece—a vivid depiction of their family under a starry sky—they were moved to tears.

"Papa, this is amazing!" Shanaya exclaimed, hugging him tightly. "You should keep doing this!"

Vivaan smiled, realizing that creativity wasn't just a form of self-expression—it was a source of healing. Through art, he found a way to process his pain and rediscover joy.

Saachi: Serendipity Sparks Renewed Purpose

For Saachi, the aftermath of the catering mishap tested her resolve. Though she had managed to salvage her relationship with the disgruntled client, the incident left her questioning whether entrepreneurship was worth the risk. There were days when she considered giving up, returning to the stability of a traditional job despite her passion for cooking.

One afternoon, while delivering snacks to a local café, Saachi encountered a young girl named Meera who worked part-time as a barista. Meera approached her shyly, holding a plate of leftover treats. "These are incredible," she said. "My mom loves sweets, but she can't afford them anymore since she lost her job. Could I buy some for her?"

Touched by the girl's sincerity, Saachi handed her a box of snacks for free. "Take these to your mom," she said gently. "And tell her I wish her well."

The next day, Meera returned with a heartfelt note from her mother, thanking Saachi for her generosity. Enclosed was a photograph of the woman smiling brightly, surrounded by the treats. Moved by the gesture, Saachi posted the photo on social media, sharing the story behind it.

To her astonishment, the post went viral, drawing attention to her business and inspiring others to support local entrepreneurs. Orders poured in from across the city, along with messages of encouragement from strangers who admired her kindness. One customer wrote, "Your food isn't just delicious—it's filled with love."

Saachi realized that her purpose extended beyond profit—it was about making a difference, however small, in people's lives. By focusing on connection rather than competition, she transformed her setbacks into stepping stones toward success.

Bharat: Finding Joy in Unexpected Places

For Bharat, the turning point came during a particularly lonely winter evening. Despite forming new friendships through his workshops, there were nights when the absence of his wife felt unbearable. He often wandered the streets of East Delhi, seeking solace in the hum of city life.

One night, as he passed a small park, he heard the sound of laughter echoing through the trees. Curious, he followed the noise and discovered a group of children playing cricket under the dim glow of streetlights. Their joy was infectious, and before he knew it, Bharat found himself cheering them on.

After the game ended, one of the boys approached him. "Uncle, do you want to join us next time?" he asked innocently.

Bharat hesitated, then nodded. "I'd like that very much."

Over the following weeks, Bharat became a regular fixture at the park, mentoring the children and sharing stories about his own childhood. In return, they taught him the rules of modern cricket, filling his evenings with laughter and camaraderie. Through these interactions, Bharat rediscovered the simple joys of play and companionship.

He also began documenting these experiences in his journal, weaving them into the memoir he had started writing months earlier. Each entry celebrated the resilience of the human spirit—the ability to find light even in the darkest corners of existence.

Moments of Illumination: Guiding Them Forward

As Vivaan, Saachi, and Bharat navigated their respective journeys, they encountered moments of illumination that reminded them of life's inherent beauty. For Vivaan, it was the act of creating art—a reminder that even amidst chaos, there is room for beauty. For Saachi, it was the kindness of strangers—a testament to the interconnectedness of all beings. And for Bharat, it was the laughter of children—a symbol of hope and renewal.

Each of them came to understand that resilience isn't about avoiding pain—it's about finding strength in vulnerability, courage in uncertainty, and light in the darkness. By shifting their perspectives, they uncovered hidden treasures within themselves and the world around them.

Chapter 14: The Ties That Bind

Human beings are not meant to walk through life alone. Our connections—with family, friends, mentors, and even strangers—are the threads that weave us into the fabric of existence. For Vivaan, Saachi, and Bharat, this chapter became a celebration of the ties that bind them to others and to themselves. Through reflection and gratitude, they came to understand that their individual journeys were never truly solitary; they were supported, guided, and uplifted by the love and kindness of those around them.

Vivaan: Rediscovering Family as a Source of Strength

For Vivaan, the realization of how deeply his family had influenced his journey came during a quiet evening at home. As he sat with Unnati and Shanaya, flipping through old photo albums, he was struck by the countless ways his loved ones had shaped him—often without him realizing it.

One photograph in particular caught his eye: a faded image of his grandmother, the woman who had first introduced him to the story of Radha. Her eyes sparkled with wisdom, and her smile radiated warmth. Vivaan remembered the hours she had spent teaching him about their ancestors, instilling in him a sense of curiosity and wonder. Though she had passed away years ago, her legacy lived on in his quest for truth and meaning.

"Do you miss her?" Shanaya asked, noticing the wistful expression on his face.

"I do," Vivaan replied softly. "But I also feel her presence sometimes—in the stories she told, in the lessons she taught me. She's still here, in a way."

This conversation prompted Vivaan to reflect on the other relationships that had sustained him throughout his life. There was Unnati, whose unwavering support had given him the courage to pursue his spiritual journey. And there was Shanaya, whose boundless enthusiasm reminded him to embrace life's simple joys. Even his colleagues, once distant and judgmental, had shown him kindness during the corporate scandal, proving that humanity often shines brightest in moments of adversity.

That night, Vivaan wrote in his journal:

"Family isn't just blood—it's the people who see your light when you forget it yourself. They remind you who you are, even when you lose sight of it."

Through this reflection, Vivaan understood that his strength didn't come from isolation but from connection. By leaning on those who loved him, he had found the resilience to face life's challenges head-on.

Saachi: Building a Community of Belonging

For Saachi, the importance of relationships became undeniable as her catering business flourished. What started as a solo venture had grown into a thriving enterprise, thanks in large part to the network of women she had met through the entrepreneurship workshop. These friendships weren't just professional alliances—they were lifelines, offering emotional support and practical advice during difficult times.

One afternoon, as Saachi prepared orders in her newly rented commercial kitchen, she noticed how seamlessly her friends worked together. Rekha handled logistics, Priya managed social media, and another friend, Sunita, coordinated deliveries. Each woman brought unique skills to the table, creating a harmonious team that operated like a well-oiled machine.

"We're unstoppable," Rekha joked as they packed boxes for an upcoming event. "Like the Avengers of snacks!"

Saachi laughed, feeling a surge of gratitude. She realized that success wasn't measured by individual achievements but by the collective impact of a united effort. By fostering a sense of belonging within her group, she had created something far greater than herself—a community rooted in trust, collaboration, and shared purpose.

Later that week, Saachi organized a small gathering to thank everyone for their hard work. Over plates of homemade delicacies, she shared a heartfelt speech:

"None of this would be possible without all of you. You've shown me that we don't have to face life's challenges alone—we can lean on each other, lift each other up, and create something beautiful together."

Her words resonated deeply, prompting tears and laughter among the group. Saachi understood then that true abundance wasn't about material wealth—it was about surrounding yourself with people who believed in you and celebrated your victories as if they were their own.

Bharat: Embracing Mentorship as a Two-Way Street

For Bharat, the ties that bound him to others took the form of mentorship—a relationship that enriched both parties equally. Through his workshops at the community center, he had formed meaningful connections with participants young and old, inspiring them to embrace their potential while learning from their perspectives.

One evening, after a particularly engaging session, Arjun approached Bharat with a thoughtful expression. "You've changed my life, sir," he said earnestly. "But I think you've learned from me too, haven't you?"

Bharat chuckled, nodding in agreement. "Absolutely. Teaching isn't a one-way street—it's a dialogue. Every person I meet teaches me something new about resilience, creativity, and hope."

This exchange reminded Bharat of the profound reciprocity of relationships. Whether it was Anjali sharing her story of loss, Arjun overcoming anxiety, or the children in the park teaching him the rules of cricket, every interaction had left an indelible mark on his heart.

Inspired, Bharat decided to expand his workshops, incorporating sessions on storytelling as a tool for healing and connection. He invited participants to share their own tales—not just of triumph but of struggle and vulnerability. Together, they created a safe space where everyone felt seen, heard, and valued.

Through these experiences, Bharat came to understand that belonging isn't about fitting in—it's about contributing to a shared narrative. By nurturing relationships built on empathy and authenticity, he had found a second family—one that filled the void left by his wife's passing.

Interconnectedness: We Are All Threads in the Same Tapestry

As Vivaan, Saachi, and Bharat reflected on their journeys, they recognized a common theme: no one is truly alone. Their individual paths were intertwined with the lives of countless others—family members, friends, mentors, and strangers whose actions rippled outward, shaping the world in ways both seen and unseen.

For Vivaan, this understanding deepened his appreciation for the infinite intelligence that connected all beings. He realized that every encounter carried purpose, whether it was a stranger's kindness or a loved one's guidance. For Saachi, it reinforced her belief in the power of community—a reminder that abundance multiplies when shared. And for Bharat, it affirmed his faith in humanity's capacity for compassion and resilience.

Each of them came to see that life's greatest gift isn't independence—it's interdependence. By embracing the ties that bind us, we unlock the fullness of our potential and discover the beauty of being part of something larger than ourselves.

Chapter 15: The Symphony of Life

Life is a symphony—a harmonious blend of highs and lows, light and shadow, joy and sorrow—all working together to create something greater than the sum of its parts. For Vivaan, Saachi, and Bharat, this chapter marked a profound awakening: the realization that their individual journeys were threads in a vast, intricate tapestry woven by the universe itself. By embracing this perspective, they discovered a deeper sense of purpose, peace, and alignment with the rhythms of existence.

Vivaan: Aligning with Universal Harmony

For Vivaan, the metaphor of life as a symphony became clear during a meditation session one quiet morning. As he focused on his breath, he visualized himself standing before an immense orchestra, each instrument representing a different aspect of his life—work, family, spirituality, creativity. At first, the music was discordant, with some instruments overpowering others and certain notes missing entirely. But as he imagined adjusting the tempo and tuning the instruments, the chaos transformed into a melody so beautiful it brought tears to his eyes.

In that moment, Vivaan understood that true fulfillment comes from achieving balance—not perfection, but harmony among all areas of life. He reflected on how far he had come: learning to trust the flow of life, prioritizing relationships over material success, and rediscovering his passion for art. Each decision, each challenge, each triumph had been a note in his personal symphony, contributing to the larger composition of his existence.

Inspired, Vivaan began applying this principle of harmony to his daily routine. He created a schedule that honored his body, mind, and soul, ensuring no single area dominated his time or energy. Mornings were reserved for meditation and journaling, afternoons for work and creative pursuits, and evenings for quality time with Unnati and Shanaya. Even small acts, like pausing to appreciate the aroma of freshly brewed chai or savoring the warmth of sunlight on his skin, became moments of gratitude and connection.

One evening, as he sat with Unnati on the balcony watching the sunset, he shared his revelation. "Do you know what I realized today?" he asked softly. "Our lives are like music. Every choice we make adds to the song we're creating. And right now, ours feels... perfect."

Unnati smiled, leaning her head against his shoulder. "I think you're right. We've finally found our rhythm."

Saachi: Embracing the Rhythm of Abundance

For Saachi, the concept of life as a symphony resonated deeply as she navigated the ebb and flow of her catering business. There were days when orders poured in, leaving her exhilarated yet exhausted, and others when things slowed down, giving her space to breathe and reflect. Initially, she viewed these fluctuations as unpredictable and frustrating. But over time, she came to see them as natural cycles—a reminder that abundance isn't constant but cyclical, much like the seasons.

One afternoon, while preparing snacks in her kitchen, Saachi noticed how seamlessly her team worked together despite the varying pace of demand. When orders surged, everyone pitched in without hesitation; during quieter periods, they used the time to innovate new recipes or strengthen their skills. It was as if they instinctively understood the importance of adapting to life's rhythm rather than resisting it.

This insight prompted Saachi to adopt a similar mindset in her personal life. She stopped viewing setbacks as failures and instead saw them as opportunities to recalibrate and grow.

Whether it was experimenting with a new dish, spending extra time with Atharv, or simply resting when needed, she embraced each phase with grace and intention.

That evening, as she tucked Atharv into bed, he asked, "Mama, why do you look so happy lately?"

Saachi kissed his forehead, smiling warmly. "Because I've learned that life is like a dance. Sometimes we move fast, sometimes slow—but every step matters. And I'm dancing to my own beat now."

Through this newfound perspective, Saachi discovered that alignment with universal principles—such as patience, gratitude, and adaptability—allowed her to navigate challenges with ease and celebrate successes with humility. Her life, once chaotic and uncertain, now flowed like a river, carrying her toward destinations she couldn't have imagined.

Bharat: Finding Balance Through Connection

For Bharat, the symphony of life revealed itself through the interconnectedness of his relationships. Over the months, he had formed bonds with people from all walks of life—young students eager to learn, seniors seeking companionship, and strangers whose paths crossed his in unexpected ways. Each interaction added depth and richness to his experience, reminding him that no one exists in isolation.

One evening, during a storytelling workshop, Bharat encouraged participants to reflect on the roles they played in each other's lives. "Think of yourselves as instruments in an orchestra," he said. "Your unique voice contributes to the harmony of the whole. Without you, the music wouldn't be complete."

The exercise sparked heartfelt conversations, with attendees sharing stories of how others had inspired, supported, or challenged them. One participant, a young woman named Priya, spoke about how Bharat's mentorship had helped her overcome self-doubt and pursue her dream of becoming a writer. Another, an elderly man named Rajiv, expressed gratitude for the friendships he had forged through the workshops, which had alleviated his loneliness.

Listening to these reflections, Bharat felt a profound sense of belonging. He realized that his purpose wasn't just to teach or guide—it was to contribute to the collective symphony of humanity. By fostering connections and nurturing relationships, he ensured that every note, no matter how small, resonated with meaning.

Later that night, as he wrote in his journal, Bharat captured this realization:

"We are all part of the same melody, playing our parts in the grand design. My role is to listen, to harmonize, and to remind others of their worth. Together, we create something extraordinary."

Harmony, Balance, and Alignment: Living in Sync with the Universe

As Vivaan, Saachi, and Bharat integrated these insights into their lives, they came to understand that harmony, balance, and alignment aren't static states—they're dynamic processes that require constant attention and adjustment. Like musicians in an orchestra, they learned to attune themselves to the cues of the universe, trusting that every note, whether joyful or painful, served a higher purpose.

For Vivaan, this meant honoring his values and staying grounded in the present moment. For Saachi, it meant embracing life's cycles and trusting in the abundance of the universe. And for Bharat, it meant fostering connections and celebrating the diversity of human experience.

Each of them recognized that life's beauty lies not in avoiding discord but in transforming it into harmony. By aligning with universal principles—love, compassion, authenticity, and resilience—they unlocked the fullness of their potential and discovered the joy of living in sync with the cosmos.

Chapter 16: The Infinite Intelligence Within

The universe speaks in whispers, but those who listen closely can hear its secrets—the timeless truths that remind us of our divine origin and purpose. For Vivaan, Saachi, and Bharat, this chapter marked the pinnacle of their spiritual awakening: the realization that they were not separate from the infinite intelligence that governs all creation. They were vessels through which the cosmos expressed itself—a living testament to the boundless potential within every human being.

Vivaan: Encountering the Life Force Once More

For Vivaan, the encounter with the infinite intelligence came during a moment of stillness at dawn. He had risen early to meditate on his balcony, gazing out at the city bathed in soft golden light. As he closed his eyes and focused on his breath, he felt the familiar presence of the life force—the energy he had first encountered months ago in Lodhi Gardens.

This time, however, the communication was more vivid, almost tangible. A voice resonated within him, clear and radiant:

"You have sought answers, Vivaan Gupta, and now you stand ready to receive them. You are not merely a participant in this symphony—you are the composer, the musician, and the music itself."

Vivaan's heart swelled with awe as the truth unfolded before him. He understood that the infinite intelligence wasn't an external entity; it was the essence of his being—the spark of divinity that animated every thought, word, and action. Every challenge he had faced, every lesson he had learned, had been orchestrated by this higher power—not to test him, but to awaken him to his true nature.

The life force continued:

"Your journey has been one of remembrance. You have remembered your connection to all things, your role in the grand design, and your ability to co-create with the universe. Trust in this knowledge, for it is eternal."

As the presence faded, Vivaan opened his eyes, tears streaming down his face. He felt an overwhelming sense of unity—not just with Unnati, Shanaya, and humanity, but with the trees, the stars, and the very air he breathed. In that moment, he knew beyond doubt that he was part of something infinitely greater than himself.

Later that day, Vivaan shared his revelation with Unnati. Though she couldn't fully grasp the depth of his experience, she sensed the transformation within him. "You seem... different," she said softly. "Like you've found what you've been searching for."

"I think I have," Vivaan replied, smiling through his tears. "I've found myself—and everything else, too."

Saachi: Realizing Her Divine Potential

For Saachi, the realization of her connection to infinite intelligence emerged during a quiet moment of gratitude. After completing a large catering order, she sat alone in her kitchen, savoring the silence. She reflected on how far she had come— from struggling to provide for Atharv to building a thriving business rooted in love and community.

As she closed her eyes and gave thanks, she felt a surge of energy course through her body—a warmth so intense it brought tears to her eyes. In that instant, she heard a whisper, gentle yet powerful:

"You are a creator, Saachi Sharma. Just as the universe brings forth galaxies, you bring forth abundance. Your thoughts shape your reality, your actions ripple outward, and your love transforms the world."

Saachi gasped, overwhelmed by the magnitude of this truth. She realized that her struggles hadn't been obstacles—they had been opportunities to tap into her innate creative power. Every decision she made, every dish she prepared, every smile she shared was an act of co-creation with the universe.

Inspired, Saachi began viewing herself not as a passive recipient of circumstances but as an active participant in shaping her destiny. She visualized her life as a canvas, painting it with intentions of joy, prosperity, and connection. To her astonishment, the universe responded swiftly, bringing new opportunities and blessings that affirmed her alignment with infinite intelligence.

That evening, as she tucked Atharv into bed, she whispered, "We're magic, beta. You and me—we create our own happiness."

Atharv grinned sleepily. "Does that mean we're superheroes?"

Saachi laughed, kissing his forehead. "Yes, beta. We're the best kind of superheroes."

Bharat: Becoming One with Universal Consciousness

For Bharat, the revelation of infinite intelligence came during a storytelling session at the community center. As he listened to participants share their experiences, he noticed a pattern—a thread of interconnectedness weaving through each story. Whether it was triumph over adversity, healing from loss, or discovering hidden talents, every narrative echoed the same underlying truth: we are all expressions of the same divine source.

After the session ended, Bharat stepped outside and gazed up at the night sky, marveling at the countless stars twinkling above. In that moment, he felt a profound sense of oneness—not just with the people he had mentored, but with the entire cosmos. A voice within him spoke, serene and infinite:

"You are the universe expressing itself as Bharat Mathur. Your joys, your sorrows, your dreams—all are threads in the tapestry of existence. Embrace this knowing, for it is the key to lasting peace."

Tears streamed down Bharat's face as he absorbed these words. He understood now that his grief over losing his wife, his loneliness, and even his moments of doubt had been integral parts of his journey—not flaws, but facets of his wholeness. By embracing his humanity, he had aligned himself with universal consciousness, becoming a conduit for love, wisdom, and compassion.

Later that night, Bharat wrote in his journal:

"I am not alone. I never was. I am the universe, and the universe is me. Together, we create, we heal, we evolve."

The Ultimate Truth: Infinite Intelligence Within Us All

As Vivaan, Saachi, and Bharat integrated these revelations into their lives, they came to understand a universal truth: infinite intelligence resides within every being. It is the silent force that guides planets, inspires art, and fuels the courage to overcome fear. By acknowledging this truth, they unlocked their full potential, stepping into roles as creators, healers, and contributors to the cosmic symphony.

For Vivaan, this meant continuing to trust the flow of life, knowing that every step he took was divinely guided. For Saachi, it meant embracing her role as a creator, using her gifts to uplift others and manifest abundance. And for Bharat, it meant celebrating his oneness with the universe, finding joy in the endless dance of existence.

Each of them recognized that their individual journeys were not isolated paths—they were chapters in the same story, written by the same hand. By aligning with infinite intelligence, they became instruments of love, harmony, and transformation, enriching the lives of everyone they touched.

Chapter 17: The Legacy of Light

A legacy is not measured by what we accumulate but by what we give—the love we share, the wisdom we impart, and the hope we ignite in others. For Vivaan, Saachi, and Bharat, this chapter marked a profound shift in perspective: the realization that their true purpose was to be vessels of light, illuminating the paths of those around them. As they reflected on their journeys, they understood that their greatest contribution to the world was not what they achieved for themselves but how they inspired others to awaken to their own infinite potential.

Vivaan: Inspiring Others Through Art and Authenticity

For Vivaan, the desire to leave a meaningful legacy crystallized during a family gathering at his parents' home. As he flipped through old photo albums with Shanaya, he noticed how intently she studied the images—her wide eyes filled with curiosity and wonder. At one point, she turned to him and asked, "Papa, will people remember you when you're gone?"

The question caught Vivaan off guard, but it prompted deep reflection. He realized that his legacy wasn't about titles, promotions, or societal approval—it was about the impressions he left on hearts and minds. It was about being remembered as someone who lived authentically, loved deeply, and shared generously.

Inspired, Vivaan decided to channel his artistic talents into creating something enduring—a series of paintings that captured the essence of his spiritual journey. Each piece depicted a pivotal moment: the lantern glowing softly in Lodhi Gardens, the cosmic energy guiding him during meditation, and the interconnectedness of all beings symbolized by a vast, starry sky. He titled the collection "Threads of Light" and hosted an exhibition at a local gallery.

To his surprise, the event drew not only friends and family but also strangers who resonated with the themes of connection, transformation, and universal consciousness. One attendee, a young man named Arnav, approached Vivaan after viewing the artwork. "Your paintings made me feel like I'm part of something bigger," he said earnestly. "Thank you for reminding me of that."

Vivaan smiled, feeling a surge of gratitude. He realized that his legacy wasn't confined to canvas—it extended to the ripple effects of his actions. By embracing authenticity and sharing his truth, he had become a beacon of inspiration for others to do the same.

That evening, as he tucked Shanaya into bed, she whispered, "Papa, your art makes people happy. That's a good legacy."

"Yes, beta," Vivaan replied, kissing her forehead. "And so is loving others the way you love me."

Saachi: Empowering Women Through Community and Compassion

For Saachi, the concept of legacy took shape through her growing network of women entrepreneurs. What had started as a small group of friends supporting each other's businesses had blossomed into a thriving community that empowered women across Delhi. Through workshops, mentorship programs, and collaborative projects, Saachi helped countless individuals overcome self-doubt, embrace their strengths, and build sustainable livelihoods.

One afternoon, as she facilitated a session on overcoming fear, a participant named Neha stood up and shared her story. "Before I met Saachi Didi, I thought my dreams were impossible," she said, her voice trembling with emotion. "But she taught me that abundance comes from within—and that we're stronger together."

The room erupted in applause, and Saachi felt tears welling in her eyes. She realized that her legacy wasn't tied to the success of her catering business—it was woven into the lives she touched. Every woman who found courage because of her example, every child whose future brightened because of their mother's empowerment, carried forward her light.

Encouraged by this realization, Saachi launched a foundation aimed at providing resources and training to underprivileged women. She named it "Shakti Rising," symbolizing the divine feminine energy within each person. Through this initiative, she hoped to create a ripple effect of empowerment, ensuring that her legacy would continue long after she was gone.

As she worked late into the night drafting plans for the foundation, Atharv peeked into her office and asked, "Mama, why do you work so hard?"

Saachi smiled, pulling him onto her lap. "Because I want to make the world brighter—for you, for everyone. And I believe we can."

Bharat: Planting Seeds of Wisdom Through Storytelling

For Bharat, the idea of legacy centered on storytelling—a medium he believed could bridge generations, cultures, and perspectives. Over the months, his workshops had evolved from simple narrative exercises to profound explorations of identity, purpose, and interconnectedness. Participants often remarked that his sessions felt less like classes and more like sacred rituals, leaving them transformed in subtle yet significant ways.

One evening, after a particularly moving session, an elderly woman named Meera approached Bharat with tears in her eyes. "You've given me back my voice," she said softly. "I thought my stories didn't matter anymore, but now I see they're part of something greater."

Bharat felt a lump rise in his throat. He realized that his legacy wasn't just the stories he told—it was the permission he gave others to tell theirs. By fostering a space where vulnerability was celebrated and authenticity was honored, he had planted seeds of wisdom that would grow and flourish in unexpected ways.

Determined to expand his reach, Bharat began compiling a book of stories shared during his workshops. Titled "Whispers of the Soul," the collection highlighted the resilience, creativity, and humanity of ordinary people facing extraordinary challenges. Proceeds from the book went toward funding educational programs for underserved communities, further amplifying its impact.

On the day of the book launch, as he signed copies for eager readers, Bharat felt a profound sense of fulfillment. He knew that his legacy wasn't confined to words on paper—it lived in the hearts of those who dared to dream, heal, and connect because of his encouragement.

Later that night, as he wrote in his journal, Bharat captured this realization:

"A legacy is not what we leave behind—it's what we pass on. My stories may fade, but the courage they inspire will endure."

The Ripple Effect: Leaving a Lasting Impact

As Vivaan, Saachi, and Bharat embraced their roles as carriers of light, they recognized that legacies are not static monuments—they are dynamic forces that evolve through time. Like ripples spreading outward from a single stone cast into water, their actions influenced countless lives, inspiring others to embark on their own journeys of self-discovery.

For Vivaan, this meant using art as a tool for awakening, reminding others of their inherent divinity. For Saachi, it meant empowering women to reclaim their power, creating a chain reaction of abundance and compassion. And for Bharat, it meant preserving stories that celebrated humanity's resilience, ensuring that wisdom endured across generations.

Each of them understood that their individual contributions were threads in the larger tapestry of existence. By aligning with infinite intelligence and embodying universal principles, they became conduits for love, harmony, and transformation—not just for themselves but for the collective whole.

Chapter 18: The Dance of Existence

Life is not a straight line; it is a spiral, a wave, a rhythm that ebbs and flows with infinite grace. For Vivaan, Saachi, and Bharat, this chapter marked a profound acceptance of life's inherent unpredictability. They realized that existence itself is a dance—a harmonious blend of chaos and order, stillness and motion, beginnings and endings. By surrendering to this flow, they discovered freedom, joy, and an unshakable trust in the universe's wisdom.

Vivaan: Embracing Uncertainty as Freedom

For Vivaan, the realization that life is a dance came during a quiet evening at home. As he watched Unnati and Shanaya laugh together over dinner, he noticed how effortlessly their interactions unfolded—each moment flowing into the next without resistance or control. It struck him that life wasn't meant to be micromanaged; it was meant to be experienced, like music or art, with room for improvisation and surprise.

This insight deepened during a meditation session later that night. As he focused on his breath, he visualized himself standing in the center of a vast, swirling vortex of energy. The movement around him was chaotic yet mesmerizing, like leaves caught in a gentle breeze. Instead of trying to stop the motion, he allowed himself to sway with it, feeling its pulse resonate within his chest.

In that moment, Vivaan understood that uncertainty wasn't something to fear—it was the essence of life itself. Every decision, every challenge, every triumph was a step in the cosmic choreography, guiding him toward greater alignment with his true nature. By embracing the unknown, he found liberation from the need to control outcomes and instead trusted in the divine timing of the universe.

The next morning, as he prepared for work, Unnati remarked, "You seem lighter today, Vivaan. Like you've let go of something."

"I think I have," Vivaan replied with a smile. "I've stopped trying to predict the steps and started enjoying the dance."

Saachi: Celebrating Growth Through Change

For Saachi, the concept of life as a dance resonated deeply as she navigated the ups and downs of her catering business and foundation. There were days when orders poured in, leaving her exhilarated yet exhausted, and others when things slowed down, giving her space to rest and reflect. Initially, she viewed these fluctuations as obstacles, but over time, she came to see them as opportunities for growth.

One afternoon, while mentoring a group of women entrepreneurs, Saachi shared her perspective on change. "Think of yourselves as dancers," she said. "Sometimes we move fast, sometimes slow—but every step adds to the rhythm of our lives. Even when the music changes, we adapt and keep moving."

Her words inspired one participant, a young mother named Sangeeta, who had been struggling to balance her ambitions with her responsibilities at home. "I never thought about it that way," Sangeeta admitted. "But maybe I don't have to wait for perfect conditions. Maybe I can start dancing now, wherever I am."

Saachi nodded, recognizing herself in Sangeeta's journey. She too had once waited for stability before pursuing her dreams, only to realize that growth happens in motion—not stagnation. By embracing change as part of the dance, she had learned to celebrate both progress and setbacks, knowing that each contributed to her evolution.

That evening, as she tucked Atharv into bed, she whispered, "Life is always changing, beta. But if we stay open, we'll find magic in every moment."

Atharv grinned sleepily. "Like magic tricks?"

"Better," Saachi replied, kissing his forehead. "Like miracles."

Bharat: Finding Joy in the Eternal Flow

For Bharat, the dance of existence revealed itself through the interconnectedness of all things. Over the months, he had formed bonds with people from all walks of life—young students eager to learn, seniors seeking companionship, and strangers whose paths crossed his in unexpected ways. Each interaction added depth and richness to his experience, reminding him that no one exists in isolation.

One evening, during a storytelling workshop, Bharat encouraged participants to reflect on their roles in the grand design. "Think of yourselves as dancers in a cosmic ballet," he said. "Your unique movements contribute to the harmony of the whole. Without you, the dance wouldn't be complete."

The exercise sparked heartfelt conversations, with attendees sharing stories of how others had inspired, supported, or challenged them. One participant, a young woman named Priya, spoke about how Bharat's mentorship had helped her overcome self-doubt and pursue her dream of becoming a writer. Another, an elderly man named Rajiv, expressed gratitude for the friendships he had forged through the workshops, which had alleviated his loneliness.

Listening to these reflections, Bharat felt a profound sense of belonging. He realized that his purpose wasn't just to teach or guide—it was to contribute to the collective dance of humanity. By fostering connections and nurturing relationships, he ensured that every step, no matter how small, resonated with meaning.

Later that night, as he wrote in his journal, Bharat captured this realization:

"We are all part of the same dance, moving to the rhythm of the cosmos. My role is to listen, to harmonize, and to remind others of their worth. Together, we create something extraordinary."

The Beauty of Uncertainty: Trusting the Flow

As Vivaan, Saachi, and Bharat integrated these insights into their lives, they came to understand that life's beauty lies not in avoiding uncertainty but in embracing it. Like dancers responding to the music, they learned to attune themselves to the cues of the universe, trusting that every twist and turn served a higher purpose.

For Vivaan, this meant honoring his values and staying grounded in the present moment. For Saachi, it meant embracing life's cycles and trusting in the abundance of the universe. And for Bharat, it meant fostering connections and celebrating the diversity of human experience.

Each of them recognized that life's rhythm isn't predictable—it's dynamic, ever-changing, and full of surprises. By aligning with universal principles—love, compassion, authenticity, and resilience—they unlocked the fullness of their potential and discovered the joy of living in sync with the cosmos.

Chapter 19: The Final Revelation

The universe speaks not only through whispers but also through thunderous revelations—moments so powerful they shatter illusions and unveil eternal truths. For Vivaan, Saachi, and Bharat, this chapter marked the pinnacle of their spiritual evolution: the realization that they were never truly separate—not from each other, not from the infinite intelligence, and not from the cosmos itself. In this final revelation, they encountered the essence of unity, dissolving the boundaries of ego and stepping into the boundless expanse of universal consciousness.

Vivaan: Dissolving the Illusion of Separation

For Vivaan, the final revelation came during a meditation retreat he attended in the serene hills of Rishikesh. Surrounded by towering mountains and the sacred flow of the Ganges River, he immersed himself in silence, seeking deeper clarity. On the third day of the retreat, as dawn painted the sky in hues of gold and pink, Vivaan sat cross-legged on a riverbank, his eyes closed, his breath steady.

As he delved deeper into stillness, he felt a surge of energy unlike anything he had experienced before. It was as if the entire universe had converged within him—a symphony of light, sound, and vibration. A voice resonated within his consciousness, vast and loving:

"You are not separate. You never were. You are me—the infinite intelligence expressing itself as Vivaan Gupta."

Tears streamed down Vivaan's face as the truth unfolded before him. He saw himself not as an isolated individual but as a thread woven into the fabric of existence. Every thought, word, and action he had ever taken rippled outward, influencing countless lives in ways both seen and unseen. He understood that his journey—the challenges, triumphs, and transformations—was part of a grand design, orchestrated by the same divine force that animated all beings.

The presence continued:

"Your search for meaning has led you back to yourself—to the realization that you are whole, complete, and infinitely connected. Trust in this knowing, for it is eternal."

When Vivaan opened his eyes, the world around him seemed transformed. The flowing river, the rustling leaves, the distant calls of birds—all vibrated with life, each element pulsing with the same energy that coursed through his veins. He realized that everything was alive, conscious, and interconnected. There was no "other"; there was only one.

That evening, as he shared his experience with fellow retreat participants, he spoke with a quiet authority that moved everyone present. "We are not alone," he said softly. "We are part of something greater than we can imagine. And when we remember this, we awaken to our true nature."

Saachi: Becoming One with the Cosmic Web

For Saachi, the final revelation emerged during a moment of gratitude after completing a large catering order for a charity event hosted by her foundation. As she stood in the bustling kitchen, surrounded by the hum of activity and the aroma of freshly prepared food, she paused to take it all in—the laughter of her team, the satisfaction of a job well done, the knowledge that her efforts would feed hundreds of families in need.

Closing her eyes, she gave thanks, feeling a warmth spread through her body—a sensation so intense it brought tears to her eyes. In that instant, she heard a whisper, gentle yet infinite:

"You are the universe expressing itself as Saachi Sharma. Your love nourishes others, your actions ripple outward, and your presence transforms the world."

Saachi gasped, overwhelmed by the magnitude of this truth. She realized that her struggles—the financial hardships, the doubts, the sacrifices—had been integral parts of her journey, not flaws but facets of her wholeness. By embracing her humanity, she had aligned herself with universal consciousness, becoming a conduit for abundance, compassion, and healing.

Inspired, Saachi began viewing herself not as a passive recipient of circumstances but as an active participant in shaping her destiny. She visualized her life as a web, each strand connecting her to others—to Atharv, to the women she mentored, to strangers whose lives she touched indirectly. To her astonishment, the universe responded swiftly, bringing new opportunities and blessings that affirmed her alignment with infinite intelligence.

That night, as she tucked Atharv into bed, she whispered, "We're magic, beta. You and me—we create our own happiness."

Atharv grinned sleepily. "Does that mean we're superheroes?"

Saachi laughed, kissing his forehead. "Yes, beta. We're the best kind of superheroes."

Bharat: Merging with Universal Consciousness

For Bharat, the final revelation came during a storytelling session at the community center. As he listened to participants share their experiences, he noticed a pattern—a thread of interconnectedness weaving through each story. Whether it was triumph over adversity, healing from loss, or discovering hidden talents, every narrative echoed the same underlying truth: we are all expressions of the same divine source.

After the session ended, Bharat stepped outside and gazed up at the night sky, marveling at the countless stars twinkling above. In that moment, he felt a profound sense of oneness—not just with the people he had mentored, but with the entire cosmos. A voice within him spoke, serene and infinite:

"You are the universe expressing itself as Bharat Mathur. Your joys, your sorrows, your dreams—all are threads in the tapestry of existence. Embrace this knowing, for it is the key to lasting peace."

Tears streamed down Bharat's face as he absorbed these words. He understood now that his grief over losing his wife, his loneliness, and even his moments of doubt had been integral parts of his journey—not flaws, but facets of his wholeness. By embracing his humanity, he had aligned himself with universal consciousness, becoming a conduit for love, wisdom, and compassion.

Later that night, Bharat wrote in his journal:

"I am not alone. I never was. I am the universe, and the universe is me. Together, we create, we heal, we evolve."

The Ultimate Truth: Infinite Intelligence Within Us All

As Vivaan, Saachi, and Bharat integrated these revelations into their lives, they came to understand a universal truth: infinite intelligence resides within every being. It is the silent force that guides planets, inspires art, and fuels the courage to overcome fear. By acknowledging this truth, they unlocked their full potential, stepping into roles as creators, healers, and contributors to the cosmic symphony.

For Vivaan, this meant continuing to trust the flow of life, knowing that every step he took was divinely guided. For Saachi, it meant embracing her role as a creator, using her gifts to uplift others and manifest abundance. And for Bharat, it meant celebrating his oneness with the universe, finding joy in the endless dance of existence.

Each of them recognized that their individual journeys were not isolated paths—they were chapters in the same story, written by the same hand. By aligning with infinite intelligence, they became instruments of love, harmony, and transformation, enriching the lives of everyone they touched.

Chapter 20: The Eternal Now

Time is an illusion—a construct of the mind that fragments the seamless flow of existence into moments we label as past, present, and future. For Vivaan, Saachi, and Bharat, this chapter marked the culmination of their spiritual awakening: the realization that life unfolds in the eternal now. By surrendering to the present moment, they discovered a timeless dimension where joy, peace, and connection are ever-present. In this state of pure presence, they encountered the divine essence of being itself.

Vivaan: Discovering Eternity in Stillness

For Vivaan, the revelation of the eternal now came during a quiet morning meditation at home. As he sat cross-legged on his balcony, gazing out at the city bathed in soft dawn light, he focused intently on his breath—the gentle rise and fall of his chest, the cool air entering his nostrils, the warmth leaving his lips. With each inhale and exhale, he felt himself sinking deeper into stillness, until the chatter of his mind dissolved into silence.

In that silence, Vivaan experienced something extraordinary: the sensation of time ceasing to exist. There was no yesterday, no tomorrow—only the boundless expanse of the present moment. He realized that every breath carried eternity within it, a direct link to the infinite intelligence that governs all creation. Each inhale was a reminder of his connection to the cosmos; each exhale was an act of surrender to its wisdom.

A voice whispered softly within him, clear and radiant:

"The eternal now is your true home. Here, you are free from fear, doubt, and longing. Here, you are whole."

Tears streamed down Vivaan's face as he absorbed these words. He understood that the key to lasting peace wasn't found in achieving goals or planning for the future—it was found in embracing the simplicity of the present moment. By anchoring himself in the now, he could access infinite possibilities, trusting that the universe would guide him toward his highest good.

Later that day, as he prepared breakfast with Unnati and Shanaya, he shared his insight. "Do you know what I realized today?" he asked gently. "Every moment is a gift. If we pay attention, we'll see that eternity is already here."

Unnati smiled, stirring a pot of chai. "That sounds beautiful, Vivaan. But how do we stay in the moment when there's so much to think about?"

Vivaan paused, then replied, "By remembering that everything we need is right here, right now. Even when life feels chaotic, the present moment is always peaceful if we choose to notice it."

Saachi: Finding Abundance in the Present

For Saachi, the concept of the eternal now emerged during a busy afternoon at her catering kitchen. Orders were piling up, deadlines looming, and stress threatening to overwhelm her. Just as frustration began to take hold, she remembered a lesson she had learned during her meditation practice: "When you feel lost, return to your breath."

Taking a deep breath, Saachi closed her eyes and centered herself. She imagined each inhale filling her with calm energy and each exhale releasing tension. To her surprise, the chaos around her seemed to soften, becoming manageable rather than overwhelming. She noticed details she hadn't before—the rhythmic chopping of knives, the sizzle of spices hitting hot oil, the laughter of her team working together. These ordinary sounds became a symphony, reminding her of the beauty hidden in everyday moments.

In that instant, Saachi realized that abundance wasn't tied to material wealth or future achievements—it was available in the present moment. Every bite of food she prepared, every smile she shared, every task completed with love was an expression of eternity. By focusing on the now, she tapped into a reservoir of gratitude and creativity that transformed her experience of work and life.

That evening, as she tucked Atharv into bed, she whispered, "Did you know that magic happens in the present moment?"

Atharv yawned sleepily. "Like what kind of magic?"

Saachi kissed his forehead, smiling warmly. "Like the magic of being alive. Of feeling the sun on your skin, tasting your favorite snack, or hearing someone laugh. All of it happens right here, right now."

Bharat: Embracing the Timelessness of Connection

For Bharat, the eternal now revealed itself through the power of human connection. During a storytelling session at the community center, he encouraged participants to reflect on the fleeting yet profound nature of their interactions. "Think of yourselves as meeting in the eternal now," he said. "This moment is all we truly have. Everything else—the past, the future—is just a thought."

The exercise sparked heartfelt conversations, with attendees sharing stories of how others had inspired, supported, or challenged them in ways that transcended time. One participant, a young woman named Priya, spoke about how Bharat's mentorship had helped her overcome self-doubt and pursue her dream of becoming a writer. Another, an elderly man named Rajiv, expressed gratitude for the friendships he had forged through the workshops, which had alleviated his loneliness.

Listening to these reflections, Bharat felt a profound sense of unity. He realized that his purpose wasn't just to teach or guide—it was to create moments of connection that transcended the constraints of time. By fostering relationships rooted in presence and authenticity, he ensured that every interaction carried the weight of eternity.

Later that night, as he wrote in his journal, Bharat captured this realization:

"The eternal now is where love lives. It is where we find each other—and ourselves. When we embrace the present moment, we step into infinity."

Living in the Eternal Now: A Gateway to Unity

As Vivaan, Saachi, and Bharat integrated these insights into their lives, they came to understand that the eternal now is not a destination—it is a practice. Like dancers responding to the music, they learned to attune themselves to the rhythm of the universe, trusting that every moment held infinite potential.

For Vivaan, this meant pausing throughout the day to savor simple pleasures—a sip of tea, a child's laughter, the warmth of sunlight on his skin. For Saachi, it meant approaching her work with mindfulness, infusing each task with love and gratitude. And for Bharat, it meant celebrating the beauty of human connection, knowing that every encounter was a sacred opportunity to express unity.

Each of them recognized that life's richness lies not in chasing after something better or waiting for conditions to improve—but in fully inhabiting the present moment. By aligning with universal principles—love, compassion, authenticity, and presence—they unlocked the fullness of their potential and discovered the joy of living in sync with the cosmos.
